P9-BZJ-809

The windshield shattered as a bullet tore through the truck.

Seth felt as though his heart had been ripped right out of his chest.

"Holly!" He twisted the wheel, putting the truck and himself between Holly and any more oncoming bullets. He was vaguely aware of the back-seat driver's side window fracturing as another bullet assaulted his vehicle.

"Holly," he said frantically, "are you hurt?"

"I'm okay!" Her voice was breathless. Shocked. Quaking.

"Stay down!"

He swerved in the street, jostled over a curb, then whipped the truck down a side street he hadn't planned on taking. The bullet had torn through the passenger seat. If Holly hadn't ducked the moment he'd said to, the bullet would've pierced her chest.

His own chest tightened at the thought and his heart beat wildly.

When he cruised into the police station parking lot, armed officers filled the space. But even here, under protection, Seth didn't feel safe...

Amity Steffen lives in northern Minnesota with her two boys and two spoiled cats. She's a voracious reader and a novice baker. She enjoys watching her sons play baseball in the summer and would rather stay indoors in the winter. She's worked in the education field for more years than she cares to count, but writing has always been her passion. Amity loves connecting with readers, so please visit her at Facebook.com/amitysteffenauthor.

Books by Amity Steffen

Love Inspired Suspense

Reunion on the Run
Colorado Ambush
Big Sky Secrets
Missing in Montana

Visit the Author Profile page at LoveInspired.com.

MISSING IN MONTANA

AMITY STEFFEN

LOVE INSPIRED SUSPENSE
INSPIRATIONAL ROMANCE

If you purchased this book without a cover you should be aware
that this book is stolen property. It was reported as "unsold and
destroyed" to the publisher, and neither the author nor the
publisher has received any payment for this "stripped book."

LOVE INSPIRED® SUSPENSE
INSPIRATIONAL ROMANCE

Recycling programs
for this product may
not exist in your area.

ISBN-13: 978-1-335-59795-3

Missing in Montana

Copyright © 2024 by Amity Steffen

All rights reserved. No part of this book may be used or reproduced in
any manner whatsoever without written permission except in the case of
brief quotations embodied in critical articles and reviews.

This is a work of fiction. Names, characters, places and incidents are either the
product of the author's imagination or are used fictitiously. Any resemblance
to actual persons, living or dead, businesses, companies, events or locales is
entirely coincidental.

For questions and comments about the quality of this book, please contact us
at CustomerService@Harlequin.com.

Love Inspired
22 Adelaide St. West, 41st Floor
Toronto, Ontario M5H 4E3, Canada
www.LoveInspired.com

Printed in U.S.A.

But Jesus beheld them, and said unto them, With men this is impossible; but with God all things are possible.
—*Matthew* 19:26

For Derek.
Thank you for your enduring patience
during my perpetual meltdowns.

ONE

Holly Nichols had ridden this route on her bike countless times before. Just about every Wednesday night since last spring, in fact. Though the shoulder was narrow, she had never felt as unsafe as she did this very moment. Some vehicles sped recklessly past her. But not the one behind her this evening. It had slowed, almost idled at one point. She knew it hadn't been following her long, perhaps only a few minutes, but she'd first spotted it sitting near her house, pulled to the side of the road, so she'd assumed the driver was texting or making a phone call.

Had they been waiting for her?

What if she hadn't left on her bike? Would they have gone after her in her own home? Home. Where her daughter was. Her heart kicked at the thought, and she longed to be home with Chloe, safe and sound. Behind locked doors.

Holly felt the opposite of safe now as her heartbeat ratcheted up several notches, and a surge of adrenaline spiked through her veins.

She took this route because she enjoyed the scenic view. It was typically calming and relaxing—the perfect backdrop for appreciating God's artistic handiwork in all its glory. The changing autumn leaves around her were brilliantly vibrant. The gorgeous river at the bottom of the ravine to her right ran parallel to the road. The water flowed quickly due to the recent rains. But she wasn't enjoying the view now.

Fear, icy and cold, slithered down her spine. Her limbs began to tingle with dread as her instincts kicked into high gear, warning her that this was not a good situation.

Yet there was nowhere for her to go. No way for her to get out of it. A feeling of helplessness seemed to strangle her.

Why didn't the driver just go around her? She had glanced over her shoulder, but with the sun beginning its evening descent behind her, she hadn't gotten a glimpse of the driver. Maybe Holly should pull over. It was possible she was just being paranoid. She should let the car pass so she could—

Her bike pitched forward as the car nudged her back tire. It was just a little bump, but that was all it took to send her careening over the edge of the road. She let out a shriek as she sped down the hill, thankfully missing the trees that were scattered about. Her heart lurched as terror seized her. She slammed on the brakes. Her tires locked, and the bike flew out from under her. Holly tumbled off a moment before her bike crashed into an oak. It hit the tree hard and bounced away in the opposite direction. She collided with the ground, rolled. Came to a stop when she hit a spongy, mossy stump.

For a second, she lay staring up at the sky—dazed, hurting and trying to comprehend what had happened.

Oh, she hurt. She hurt everywhere.

Right. She had been hit. In that moment, with her limbs already throbbing, she was infinitely grateful for the helmet she wore.

Someone had hit her with their car.

On purpose.

Who? Why? Where were they now?

Those thoughts got her moving.

Quickly.

A car door slammed.

Groaning from the pain ricocheting through her body, she scrambled to her feet and stumbled forward, darting behind a thick spruce tree. She leaned into it for support, hiding behind it as she peered up the incline. It was a struggle to see through the foliage.

Through the thick layer of pine boughs, she could make out a pair of black work boots.

She wanted desperately to believe whoever had hit her had stopped to help. But she couldn't deny that the nudge off the road wasn't an accident. So no, whoever hit her hadn't stopped to help. Had they stopped to finish her off? Fear shimmied through her at the thought.

"Come out, come out wherever you are." The man's voice was gravelly. "I'm going to find you one way or another."

Not a chance. Please God, protect me.

Her breath came in frantic little bursts. Her body buzzed, and she wasn't sure if it was from pain or fear.

What was she going to do? Where was she going to go? She couldn't go back up to the road. Not when the stranger stood guard. She couldn't run along the length of the river, not without being spotted. Once she moved from where she stood, partially covered, he would see her for sure.

She felt so trapped. Caught. A whimper of fear tried to creep up her throat. She locked it inside, afraid of giving herself away. A million frantic, overlapping prayers coursed through her mind as she begged God for protection. For a way out.

The boot-clad feet took a few steps down the hill, dry leaves crunching beneath the man's weight. "I know you're down there."

Holly's heart beat so fast, so hard, she could hear her blood pulsing through her veins, sloshing in her ears. Her entire body vibrated with terror.

Oh, please God, please.

It was a quiet road, but she prayed for a vehicle to come along. Or maybe not. What would he do to a passerby?

A gunshot split the air, taking her by surprise and startling a shriek free from her chest. She slapped a hand over her mouth, but it was too late.

The man laughed. The sound was grating and sent a fresh spear of terror ripping through her.

Instinctively, she knew she had given herself away.

Adrenaline made her oblivious to the injuries she'd sustained in her crash. There was no choice. She shot from her hiding place and bolted straight toward the river, unbuckling her helmet as she ran, afraid the bright pink color would give her away once she hit the water. She tossed it aside.

A second shot echoed through the air.

Please God, oh please...

Bark splintered, showering from a tree directly to her left. She swerved, continuing her plea to God, and kept moving. Another shot rang out and chunks of earth slapped against the back of her legs as she wove through the foliage. She burst from the vegetation, reaching the river's edge.

For just a moment she was airborne as she leaped into the water. She plunged into its icy depths. Her already banged-up knees scraped along the rocky bottom. She didn't fight the current but let it carry her. While the water was moving along at a rapid pace, the riverbed wasn't terribly deep. Her body was dragged along the bottom, bumping over rocks and debris.

She held her breath until her lungs ached.

Until her head felt as though it might explode.

Until she knew she would pass out if she didn't take a breath.

Finally, unable to withstand another second submerged, she pushed up with her toes. Her head broke through the surface and she gasped, sucking in the cool evening air. She swiveled her neck, allowing the current to carry her around a bend. The man was nowhere in sight. But she wasn't sure how far behind he was.

Was he going to come after her?

She had no idea but thought it likely.

The river continued to move her along, taking her away from the threat as her mind scrambled to come up with a plan. She rounded another bend and reached out, latching on to the branch of a fallen tree. With a great bit of effort and a little bit of stumbling, she pulled herself to standing. The water swirled around her, waist-deep, as the tree held her in place. She carefully edged herself along the trunk, moving toward the shore. The current tugged at her, and without the tree bracing her, she knew she would be swept along.

Her body felt like lead as she inched forward, each step an effort. One shoe was lost in the tumult, and the bare foot squished along the mucky bottom. When she reached the edge, she managed to clamber up the muddy embankment. Her entire body shook from exertion, fear and cold, but she was grateful to have escaped.

Thank You, dear Lord.

She stood still for a moment, relieved to be on solid ground. Her lungs heaved as they sucked in air. The hammering of her heart was so intense it felt as if it was about to pound its way out of her chest. Her head swam as she tried to wrap her mind around what had just happened. Every inch of her body ached, having been tossed around and battered.

She was cold. So very cold that her teeth clattered together, creating a rhythmic chattering.

But she was alive, and in that moment, that was what mattered.

Patting her pocket, she realized her phone was gone. No doubt torn away by the current. Not that it mattered. It hadn't been waterproof and would've been no help now, anyway.

Her energy was sapped, and she was tempted to flop onto her back, let her exhaustion overtake her. But she couldn't afford that small luxury. It was imperative to keep moving. Putting one foot in front of the other, she headed away from the river. The droning sound of a car engine drifted through the air.

The Mulberry River ran more or less adjacent to the road, though it meandered into the forest and then back out again. She couldn't be too far off if she could hear a vehicle passing by.

With great care she trudged onward, trying to stay vigilant in case her attacker had somehow tracked her down. She didn't know how he could. He would have no way of knowing how far the river had carried her. She'd guess she'd gone half a mile or more.

Perhaps he'd even assume the river had claimed her life.

His voice… *Come out, come out wherever you* are played on a repetitive loop in her mind. That laugh, raspy and malicious, sent terror coursing through her. Did she know that voice? She didn't think so. But had he disguised it? The tone was teasing, lilting, yet hard and cold.

Who was he?

Did he know who she was?

Was this a random attack?

No. He'd been sitting outside of her home, so she didn't think so. Yet she couldn't be sure. Maybe he'd seen her leave on her bike and decided she was an easy target.

Her legs burned as she made her way up the steep incline. She was used to physical activity, but the ordeal had taken a toll on her body. She was panting, sweating, hurting by the time she reached the road.

Heart hammering, knees wobbling, she stood in the tree line watching for traffic.

Would her assailant go cruising by? Was he still searching for her at the site of her crash? Had he already hightailed it out of the area? Or had he jogged along the riverbank, trying to find her? The current had moved swiftly, so it would take him a while to catch up.

Holly glanced over her shoulder as paranoia hit her hard. No one was sneaking through the trees behind her.

A vehicle to the west, the direction she'd come from, caught her eye. Was it him?

Her staccato breaths were so sharp they ached.

No.

The man who had hit her had been driving an older sedan. The vehicle heading her way was a big black truck.

For just the briefest instant she worried that her attacker had an accomplice, but then she realized she had to take a chance. The hike up the hill had drained her. The nearest house was miles away. She didn't think she'd be able to make it there.

Gathering her courage, she stumbled out of the woods, waving her arms and saying yet another silent prayer.

* * *

Seth Montgomery slammed his foot against the brake pedal. The tires squealed and the truck fishtailed. The woman who'd staggered onto the slim shoulder of the road held out her hands as if begging him to stop. His heart thumped hard against his chest, and his entire body buzzed with the realization that if he hadn't been paying attention, he could have plowed right over her.

What was she thinking? Stepping in front of a moving vehicle like that—

That thought was cut short as he noticed her appearance, her frantic movements.

She was in complete disarray. Her dark, shoulder-length hair was sopping wet, plastered to her head like a helmet. Drenched clothes clung to her body. Her athletic pants were shredded at the knees, and blood spread out through the pale pink fabric.

She was missing a shoe.

What in the world?

He reached for his door handle. His frustration fizzled away and turned into alarm as he darted around the front of the truck.

"What happened to you? Are you okay?" The words shot out as his gaze raked over her, assessing. "What can I do to help?"

"I was riding my bike." Her eyes scanned the road. She was trembling. Clearly terrified. "Someone hit me."

"A hit-and-run?" His ire flared.

She glanced at him then, their eyes locking, and he felt himself sway as he was mentally transported back in time. It was as if the world tilted, knocking him off balance. His breath caught.

"Holly?" His tone sounded raspy in his own ears.

Holly Nichols had been his first love. His only love,

really. She'd been his high school sweetheart, and she'd broken his heart over a decade ago. He often blamed his single status on the military. It was tough to meet someone when you were enlisted, facing deployments and gone for long stretches of time.

Yet deep down he knew that was just an excuse. Plenty of military men were family men. He simply wasn't one of them.

She blinked, as if focusing on him for the first time, too. "Seth."

Seeing her again evoked a maelstrom of emotions within him. None of which he felt like dealing with in that moment.

As it turned out, he didn't have time to delve into the past. The current situation was far more demanding.

"Someone hit you and took off?"

She shook her head, and water droplets sprayed them both. "Yes. No. I mean, hitting me was deliberate. But he didn't take off. At least not right away. He got out of his car and shot at me. I had to jump in the river. It was the only way to escape. I managed to climb out and ended up here."

Her gaze skittered down the quiet road, and fear danced across her lovely features.

"What?" Now he glanced around, hyperaware, watchful for approaching trouble. How long had they been standing out here in the open? Not long, but he wasn't going to wait around for another second. He gently grabbed her arm and ushered her to the passenger door. He opened it for her, then because she seemed about ready to topple, he hoisted her inside. Slamming the door, he darted around the truck.

By the time he had dropped back into the driver's

seat, she had buckled her seat belt. She twisted around and looked out the back window.

"Are you hurt?"

She looked terribly banged up, but she was able to move on her own, so he was going with the assumption that nothing was broken.

"I'm fine." She was still twisted around, watching over her shoulder, studying the road through his back window. "Did you pass a car? A silver one, or maybe it was gray, parked on the side of the road?"

He frowned even as he put the truck in gear again.

"No. I didn't see anyone on the side of the road." He paused a second, trying to think. "A car did pass me though, going the other direction. I wasn't really paying attention." He had other things on his mind, like the argument he'd just had with his brother, Eric. They rarely argued, so this disagreement had left Seth rattled. No time to think of that now. "But it might have been silver. Either way, whoever pushed you off the road was gone. I've been driving this road for miles and never saw anyone parked along the side."

He cast a quick look her way as they took off. She was facing forward now, biting her lip. Her hands were clenched into fists, and chill bumps had broken out over her arms.

She was probably in shock.

Her teeth began to chatter so loudly he thought her jaw must ache.

For sure she was freezing. The evening air was chilly, and the river had to have been frigid.

He cranked up the heat, then swiveled all the vents her way.

"I'll get you to the police station. Or the hospital. Maybe the hospital," he decided, muttering to himself.

She whipped around to face him, as if his words had pulled her back to reality. "No, I need you to take me home." Her voice trembled. "Please."

"I don't think—"

"Please, my daughter is there. She's only five. She's with her teenage babysitter. That man was clearly after me. I need to make sure Chloe is safe. The car was sitting outside my house. Whoever he is, he knows where I live. What if he goes back there to wait for me? I need to get to my daughter. Now."

Her daughter.

He ignored the jolt his heart gave. Of course Holly was married by now. Unlike him, she'd moved on, started a family. The terror in her tone rattled him. Perhaps after an eight-year stint in the Marines, and two tours in Afghanistan, he was a bit jaded. If someone was malicious enough to run Holly off the road, then shoot at her, he didn't doubt they'd be unscrupulous enough to go after a child.

He handed her his phone and stepped on the gas. "You probably know reception isn't great out here. But try to call 911. Have them go to your house. We'll meet them there. They might even get to your daughter before we do."

After several attempts she slapped the phone against her thigh. "Nothing is going through."

"Give it a minute. As soon as we crest that hill up ahead, we should get reception again."

Did they have a minute? Did Chloe?

"How far away do you live?"

"We're only about four miles away." She studied his phone impatiently. Her grip around it was so tight that her knuckles were white. "You have more bars now."

He stayed silent as she placed the emergency call,

quickly explained what had happened and emphatically begged them to send someone to her house immediately.

As she rattled off her address, he recognized the name of the road. They were close, would probably make it there before any officer would.

Please God, let her little girl be safe.

It was bad enough someone had attacked Holly, but the thought he may go after a child made Seth livid.

Usually one to abide by the law, he broke the speed limit racing to the address Holly had given to the dispatcher. He figured God and the authorities would for sure grant him some grace in this situation, given that a child's life may be on the line.

The closer they got to Holly's address, the more agitated she became. She made whimpering noises. Her lips moved, and her hands were folded tightly in her lap. He thought, perhaps, scattered somewhere in there were a few prayers.

He asked softly, "Are you praying?"

She turned to him, and her pained expression sent arrows through his heart.

"Yes, I am."

He nodded, not knowing what to say, but mentally filing it away as another thing that had changed since they'd last seen each other.

"Do you have any idea who attacked you?" He realized he should focus on the issue at hand.

She hesitated, and he wasn't sure if she was thinking it over or unwilling to be honest.

"I don't know."

"We're almost there." He slowed just enough to take a sharp turn onto a dirt road.

"It's the second mailbox on the left."

They were in a rural, wooded area. Mailboxes were

dotted up and down the road, but the lots were large and private.

He whipped into her driveway and rounded the curve that cut off the view of the house from the road.

A beat-up silver car was parked haphazardly right in front of the attached garage.

Holly let out a strangled sound that twisted his heart into knots. "That's the car. The one that ran me off the road."

He skidded to a stop behind the vehicle, blocking it in. Holly unbuckled her seat belt and opened the door. He latched on to her arm, held her in place. She was in no condition to be jumping out of a vehicle and chasing after a gunman.

"Stay here," he ordered as he slammed the truck into Park.

She didn't even look his way. Tugging her arm from his grip, she shoved the door open and leaped onto the driveway. She stumbled, almost fell, but righted herself and kept going.

He burst from the truck and tore after her. They raced toward the front door.

A scream split the air, stopping them both.

"Chloe!" Holly cried, her terror piercing his heart.

In unison they changed trajectory and raced around the house, desperate to reach the backyard.

TWO

Holly gasped in horror as they rounded the corner of the garage.

Melanie, her teenage babysitter, let out another piercing shriek as she pounded her small fist against the back of the man pulling Chloe from the playhouse built into her swing set. The middle rung of the ladder busted under his weight, sending splinters flying. His body twisted as the support gave way. He landed in a stumble as he jerked Chloe free, tightly holding her with one arm.

"Mel, no!" Holly ran toward the melee, fearful of what the man would do to the small teen. Every inch of her body ached and throbbed from being thrashed in the river, but she dashed across her enormous backyard, fully intending on ripping her child from the stranger's arms.

Seth charged past her.

Melanie pivoted around. Her eyes were huge, but her relief was palpable when she saw them. She tore off, running toward the house, clearly terrified.

Holly's only thought was to get to her daughter, but in that split second Seth seemed to skid to a stop. His arm flung up, slamming into Holly's chest, effectively stopping her in place as well. Fear sizzled through her in that instant because she realized immediately why Seth was holding her back.

"I'll shoot." The stranger held her squirming, screaming daughter in one arm and a gun in the other hand. "I will shoot!"

Despite the chaos of the moment, Holly had enough wherewithal to be grateful that the man was aiming the gun at her and not her child.

But Chloe, in the midst of a full-on meltdown, didn't seem to care that the man had a gun. She was far too young to understand what the implications of that were. She was fearful of strangers and screaming for her momma.

Thrashing.

Kicking.

The man was clearly struggling to hold her as she writhed in his arms.

"Stay back." Seth's tone held a low warning, as if he knew it was taking every ounce of her self-control not to race toward her child, despite the imminent danger.

Holly whimpered and hated how helpless she felt in that moment.

"Just put her down." Seth shouted to be heard over Chloe. "Put her down and walk away."

The man grinned and started walking backward. "I'll walk away, all right. But I ain't putting her down."

Holly glanced around the yard, trying to determine what she could use as a weapon. She spotted her shovel still leaning against the gardening shed, where she'd rested it after planting a spruce tree last night. There was no way she could dart over to grab it. Even if she did, it was no match for a gun. She didn't doubt the man would follow through on his threat.

"Take me instead." Holly took a step forward, but

didn't dare go any farther without the man's permission. "I'll go willingly."

"Now, there's a thought," he replied. "You should've let me take you by the river. But no. You had to make things difficult. So it's come to this."

Holly didn't get the chance to argue her point.

Chloe threw herself back with all her tiny, angry might. She smashed the back of her head into the man's face, leaving him with an instantly bloody nose. The man cried out in pain and dropped Chloe as his hands flew to his face. She thudded to her feet, then landed in a belly flop. A deafening wail erupted from her mouth.

Seth moved faster than Holly thought humanly possible. He was on the man in an instant, tackling him. Taking him down.

She was vaguely aware of the sound of sirens in the distance, growing closer with each breath she took.

Holly rushed to Chloe and scooped the girl into her arms. Relief flooded over her. Her daughter was safe, in her embrace, and she didn't ever want to let her go.

She whirled just in time to see Seth yank the gun from the man's hand. The stranger slammed a meaty fist into Seth's sternum, then gave Seth a shove. The gun went flying as Seth lost his grip on it. Seth returned the blow, but the man—who was large, bulky and looked as though he spent most of his days in a gym—managed to shake Seth off.

Then the two were on their feet, circling each other in a dangerous dance.

Her heart pounded, and dread spilled through her. She wanted to help but didn't know what she could do.

Almost too fast for Holly to comprehend, the man pulled an object from his pocket. In an instant, a blade sprang into place. The man swung, and though Seth jumped backward, Holly's heart nearly exploded when he let out a grunt of pain. Then red began oozing from Seth's side, spreading out through the fabric of his gray thermal shirt.

The man grinned cruelly and swiped again, but this time Seth managed to dodge him.

The sirens were louder now, a cacophony of noise drawing close, announcing multiple vehicles.

Holly locked eyes with the attacker for the briefest of moments, but it was long enough to burn his face into her memory. His pale blue eyes were cold, empty of emotion, and in that instant Holly knew if not for the police who were likely spilling into her yard at that very moment, he wouldn't think twice about killing all three of them if he had the chance.

Instead, he grabbed the gun he'd lost hold of and took off running.

Seth moaned, then staggered, his hand pressed against his wound. Blood seeped through his fingers. Holly's entire body tingled with dread, anxiety and adrenaline.

The sound of gravel crunching in her driveway brought her a modicum of relief. Then doors slammed.

"Back here!" Holly shouted. "We need help!"

Holly moved toward Seth, though Chloe had a stranglehold on her neck. As she slid an arm around his waist, careful not to put pressure on his wound, he leaned into her. It felt more like an embrace than an acceptance of support.

Though he was injured, he was standing, and his weight pressed against her was comforting. Seth had always made her feel safe, secure.

"He got away." His voice was nearly a growl. "I can't believe I let him get away." He glared off into the woods, as if tempted, even in his injured state, to go after the man.

"But you stopped him from taking Chloe." Gratitude nearly overwhelmed her. If Seth hadn't rushed forward, hadn't attacked the man, hadn't fought him off... She slammed a door on those thoughts and concentrated on the moment. "Thank you."

One of the French doors that led to her back deck opened. Melanie poked her head out. She still looked terrified. "I called the police! They're here!"

That much was obvious, but Holly only nodded, knowing the police had already been on their way. Still, she appreciated Melanie's effort and quick thinking. The teen slammed the door shut again and disappeared.

As officers darted around the house, coming into view, Holly felt a sense of relief, but it was short-lived. She wondered what the chances were that this was over. The answer was clear—they didn't seem likely at all.

Ignoring the pain in his side, Seth strode down the hospital hallway in search of Holly and her daughter. He had been sufficiently numbed and stitched up, though he'd refused painkillers because he didn't want his thinking to grow fuzzy.

He was irritated with himself for not anticipating the attacker's move but grateful he had managed to leap out of the way. While the knife wound was long, it hadn't been deep enough to cause severe damage. Still, being checked over and sitting through fifteen stitches had taken more time than he liked. He was thankful for the change of clothes he kept in a duffel bag in the back of his truck. Life on the ranch could get messy, but it had never come in quite as handy as it had today. He could only imagine the looks he'd have gotten if he'd trudged through the hallways in his blood-soaked clothing.

It was difficult to ignore the cloying scent of the hospital, the warring combination of illness and cleanliness. He hadn't been in a hospital since his older sister, Ella, had succumbed to cancer several years ago. If he could've avoided it tonight, he would have. But the emergency crew that showed up at Holly's was insistent that he needed stitches, which they couldn't administer. And he'd known they were right.

He wanted to know how Holly was doing. While she and her daughter appeared fine, the EMTs on-site had suggested they also go to the ER to be checked out. Out of concern for her daughter, Holly had agreed.

Seth thought they were most likely both okay, but he needed to see for himself.

How ironic he had left his house this evening in an effort to clear his head after a rare but intense disagreement with his brother. Now here he was, his mind whirling, his thoughts spinning in seemingly a thousand different directions.

Seeing Holly after all these years would've thrown him for a loop under the best of circumstances. She'd nearly been killed tonight. He couldn't get the sight of her—bedraggled, terrified, stumbling onto the road—out of his head.

He had so many questions.

Who was after her?

Was it a random act? He didn't think so.

Why would they want her daughter?

He had other questions, and while he knew the answers were none of his business, he couldn't help but wonder.

Was she married?

Divorced?

Widowed?

At some point he had realized she wasn't wearing a

ring. He was frustrated with himself for noticing, but what did that mean? Did she lose it in the river? Take it off before taking a bike ride?

Who was Chloe's father?

Where was he?

On a business trip?

Or not part of their lives?

The girl looked nothing like her mother. Holly had chestnut hair, creamy skin and eyes the color of dark-roasted coffee. Chloe had a smattering of freckles, honey-colored hair and wild corkscrew curls. Her eyes were green. Did she look like her father? She must.

Stop. Just stop, he mentally chastised himself. After what had gone down tonight, Holly's personal life should be the least of his concerns.

He reached the private waiting room he'd been searching for and knocked. A quick, hard, sharp sound.

"Come in," called a vaguely familiar masculine voice.

Seth entered the room, a small, private waiting area for families and friends of patients. Now it was being used for questioning.

"Am I interrupting?" Seth asked, even though a nurse had told him his presence had been requested in room 102.

Detective Mateo Bianchi, whom Seth had met this past spring when his brother was going through a challenging time, motioned for Seth to take a seat in the only extra chair in the room. The detective sat in another chair, and Holly sat on the industrial-looking sofa.

Alone.

"Where's Chloe? Is she okay?"

"She's fine, Seth." Holly sounded worn and looked understandably weary. "She has some scrapes on her knees and palms from the tumble she took. They were made all better by some pretty, flowered bandages."

Seth knew what she wasn't saying. It could have been so much worse.

Thank You, Lord.

The thought startled him, especially when he realized he'd reached out to Him more than once tonight. It wasn't as if speaking to God was a foreign concept. But it was certainly a rusty one. The realization hit him with a wave of shame. While he'd drifted from his faith the past several years, he'd never strayed completely. Still, the knowledge that He had protected them all tonight hit him hard.

He was humbled by the realization and knew he had so much to be grateful for.

"She's with Officer Lainie Hughes," Holly continued, mentioning the only female officer that had been on the scene at her house. "I didn't think Chloe should be part of the questioning, but she refused to go with any of the male officers. She's already pretty rattled. While I hated leaving her, at least I know she's safe in a room just down the hall."

"I'm glad to hear it." Seth sank into the chair across from Holly. He winced, noting that her cheek was slightly swollen, and a purplish bruise had set in. Her hands had small nicks and scrapes, probably from the riverbed. The tumble down the hill and jostling in the river could have resulted in shattered bones. A concussion. Had the current been any stronger, she could have died.

That thought was like a gut punch.

As much as he hated seeing her face bruised, he sent up yet another prayer of thanksgiving, so grateful that for the most part she was okay.

"And you, Seth?" Detective Bianchi asked.

"Just a few stitches." Fifteen was a bit more than a few, but he didn't want to take any attention away from the matter at hand. "Don't suppose you caught the guy?"

"Unfortunately not." The detective frowned. "The vehicle he left behind was stolen. We're checking for prints, but I don't have high hopes that it will lead us anywhere. Holly mentioned he wore leather gloves."

Seth nodded and sagged into the chair, trying to get comfortable now that his gash had started to throb again.

"We're just wrapping up questioning," Detective Bianchi said. "Then I'd like to hear your side of events."

Seth sat forward. "Should I leave to let you finish?"

Holly shook her head. "I don't mind if you stay."

Relieved, he relaxed and leaned back again.

"You said you didn't recognize your attacker." The detective's attention was on Holly. "But do you know of anyone who would be holding a grudge against you? Any idea who sent him?"

Holly raked a hand through her tangled hair. She had changed into dry clothes before they headed to the hospital, but her hair was still damp. "Working as a forensic accountant, I could probably give you a page full of people who are holding grudges. I've uncovered Ponzi schemes, money laundering, fraudulent billing practices, one partner swindling another." She shrugged. "My work has resulted in a handful of people serving time, as you know. So, yes, I can think of more than a few people who would be holding a grudge." She pulled in a shuddering breath, her eyes filling with tears. "I never imagined my work could ever put Chloe at risk."

Detective Bianchi leaned forward and patted Holly's knee. It was a brief but friendly gesture and took Seth by surprise.

"It's okay, Holly. We don't know that this is work-related at this point. But we *will* catch whoever is behind this. You have my word."

"Thank you, Mateo."

"Do you two know each other?" Seth was curious about the familiarity that seemed to flow between them.

"We're acquaintances. We've worked together. The department has hired my services in the past."

Detective Bianchi nodded his agreement. "I'll look back on our records, see if any of the cases stand out. You do the same."

So Holly was a forensic accountant and even worked with local law enforcement. Seth was only momentarily surprised by that. Holly had been smart, the top of her class, and had always made the honor roll. She'd been president of Math Club and on the debate team. Yet she had also been from a poor family and had not planned on going to college because she hadn't thought it possible.

Something must have changed. Clearly she'd gotten a degree and had a good career. She had come a long way, and it reminded him how many years were now between them. Seth was happy for her.

"I'd like a list, no matter how long, of possible suspects," Detective Bianchi said.

"I can do that."

"Any jilted exes?" he pressed.

Holly's eyes flickered to Seth. His jaw clenched, and she quickly looked away.

"No. I don't date." She shifted in her seat, as if the topic made her uncomfortable. "Right now, I'm entirely devoted to my daughter."

Detective Bianchi hesitated a beat. His eyes darted from Holly to Seth and back again. "Tell me what I'm missing."

"It's nothing." Holly waved her hand dismissively. "Really."

"Let me be the judge of that."

"We dated," Seth said, so that Holly wouldn't have to. She darted a glance at him but quickly looked away. "Ages ago. A lifetime ago. Back in high school, to be exact."

"Given the nasty gash on your side, I think it's safe to say I won't be adding you to the suspect list." He leveled his gaze on Holly again. "What about Chloe's father? Are you on good terms with him?"

"I don't know who he is," Holly stated.

Seth felt his eyebrows hitch. Holly noticed, and she scowled at him.

"Chloe is adopted." Pointedly ignoring Seth, she directed her answer toward the detective. "She's been with me for nearly three years. Her mother passed away while Chloe was in my care, as a foster child. Her mother lived a very troubled life and didn't know who Chloe's father was."

Adopted. Seth realized that would explain the complete difference in their looks. While the news should surprise him, he found it didn't. Holly had always had a caring nature. She had also wanted a house full of kids.

"All right." The detective jotted something in his notebook. "Anyone else come to mind? Disgruntled coworkers? Anyone from Chloe's past?"

Holly shook her head. "I got to know her mother. There's no one from Chloe's past that sticks out. I get along with my coworkers, other than some normal irritations, I suppose." Then her eyes widened. "I'm so frazzled I didn't think of this before. But I received a phone call this morning. It seemed strange, but I've had stranger."

"Go on, I'm listening."

Seth sat forward. He was listening, too.

"It was a woman. She wouldn't give her name. She called from a blocked number and was insistent that I meet with her. Tomorrow." Holly tugged her hand through her hair again, a nervous habit Seth recognized from all those years ago. "She wanted to meet as soon as possible, but I was booked up today. She said the meeting had to be in person so she could give me something. She asked if I could meet at eleven. She suggested the park on the edge of town."

"That seems more than a little strange," Mateo said.

Holly shrugged. "You wouldn't believe some of the inquires I get. Just last week I had someone call to ask if I could go over their deceased grandmother's finances because they thought their inheritance should have been bigger. They accused their aunt of stealing some of the funds. I've had more than a few jilted exes ask me to look into finances after a divorce because they were convinced money was being hidden from them. I could go on. But I assure you, while a bit unusual, I wasn't alarmed by the call." She frowned. "But now the timing seems questionable to me."

"Maybe someone doesn't want you to go to that meeting tomorrow."

Holly's eyes filled with tears, and Seth wished he'd kept his mouth shut. The poor woman had been through a lot tonight and was clearly at her breaking point. There was no need for him to point out the obvious.

"Do you remember anything else about the call?" Mateo pressed.

Her brows furrowed. "She did say I came highly recommended. She didn't say who recommended me, and I didn't think to ask."

"We'll catch them, Holly." Mateo's voice was firm. "Maybe not tonight. But we'll catch them." He turned to Seth. "Are you ready to tell me your side of events?"

"Sure." But his mind was on Holly and her daughter. He could feel the fear emanating off her. His heart seemed to twist in his chest, and he was painfully aware that she had come close to dying tonight.

She's not your responsibility.

Yet while he began answering the detective's questions, he silently vowed that he would do whatever he had to do to keep Holly and Chloe safe. His heart wouldn't allow him to make any other choice.

Holly stood in her darkened living room, looking out at the night between the crack in her curtains. Though she was wide-awake she couldn't bear the thought of leaving the lights on in her house. What if her attacker was in the woods? Even with curtains closed, she worried he'd find a way to peer inside.

Office Joe Rollins had driven her and Chloe home. He was now parked in her driveway, keeping watch. She knew him, but not well. He had graduated high school a year ahead of her and Seth. He'd been on the football team with Seth, but they'd been more acquaintances than friends.

Still, Seth's comment that he was a "good guy" when Detective Bianchi mentioned he'd be on overnight duty didn't really calm her nerves. Though she was grateful for the presence of law enforcement, she was too rattled to relax.

Her mind kept playing over the night's events on a constant loop. She could have died tonight. Chloe had almost been kidnapped. Chloe meant the world to Holly, and she couldn't imagine life without her.

Then there was Seth.

Seth.

Her heart kicked in her chest at the thought of him. She'd never expected to see him again. They hadn't ended on good terms years ago, something she took full responsibility for. To this day she regretted how abruptly, how callously she had ended their relationship.

He had deserved better.

Yet he had risked himself to save her and Chloe and had ended up getting injured in the process. Stabbed. She was so grateful the Lord had been watching over them all tonight. She had grown up not knowing of His love, His mercy and protection. But she relished her faith now, relied on it always.

Her breath shuddered as she tried not to picture the blood as it had spread over Seth's fingers. He'd tried to act tough, but Holly knew him well enough, even after all this time, to notice the slight way he winced when he shifted position. She'd observed the hitch in his breath when he'd stood too fast after questioning.

Had she even properly thanked him? She wasn't sure. The evening had been such a whirlwind of activity and emotions that she could hardly recall the specifics. But there was one thing she knew.

It was only by the grace of God that they had all been spared.

Chloe cried out in her sleep from her bedroom down the hall. Holly stepped away from the window, feeling the need to comfort her, even if she hadn't awakened. Her daughter had been through so much trauma already in her young life. All Holly wanted to do was love and protect her. How had she ended up putting her life in danger?

As she hurried through the dark house, she knew that

officer in the driveway or not, she wouldn't be able to sleep a wink.

Not when her attacker was out there.

Most likely just waiting to strike again.

THREE

Seth tugged open the door of the cruiser sitting in Holly's driveway. The interior light didn't turn on, which he knew was a safety feature. He dropped onto the passenger seat, grimacing at the biting pain that erupted from the gash in his side.

"I figured you weren't going to take no for an answer," Officer Joe Rollins said wryly.

"You figured right."

"You do know you shouldn't be here, right? There's paperwork that needs to be done for ride-alongs."

"Are we going somewhere?" Seth's tone oozed innocence. "No? I didn't think so. I'm not really riding along. I'm just sitting here."

Joe shook his head, not looking the least bit happy with Seth's logic.

They had never really been friends, but they had gotten along just fine back in high school. After contacting some old acquaintances, Seth had managed to track down Joe's cell phone number. He had called the officer to tell him his plan.

Seth had permission to park at Melanie's parents' place next door. He'd then sneak through the woods, so as not to draw anyone's attention, and help Joe keep watch. Joe had tried to dissuade him, but Seth wasn't having it.

He had known there was no way he was going to be able to sleep when Holly and her daughter could be in danger. He told himself it had nothing to do with their history. If she had been a stranger flagging him down, he'd be worried then, too.

Yet he wasn't fooling himself. The fact that it was Holly at risk sent his heart galloping every time he tried to relax. When he closed his eyes, he couldn't stop picturing her bruised face, couldn't stop envisioning the terror in her eyes when she'd stepped out on the road in front of him.

It was not possible to just pack up those memories and pretend he could get on with his life, no looking back.

Which was why he'd come up with a plan.

It maybe wasn't the best plan, but it was all he had, so he'd gone with it.

Now here he was, sitting in a cruiser in her driveway in the middle of the night, chatting up the officer assigned to keep her safe.

"Look, I spent eight years in the Marines." Seth's tone had gone deadly serious. "I don't plan on getting in your way, but I assure you, I know how to handle myself. I will *not* be a liability. I just need to be sure that Holly is safe. You didn't see the look in that man's eyes tonight. He would've killed her outright. I'm sure of it. Maybe even her little girl. No way can I go home, curl up in my cozy bed and get any sleep. You get what I'm saying?"

Joe hesitated a beat. "Yeah, I get it. I've been there. Situations like that, it can be impossible to turn off your mind." He sighed. "I actually don't mind the company. It's just that I think nothing's going to happen tonight. It's unlikely the suspect would be back so soon. Besides, the whole idea of a cruiser in the driveway is to be a deterrent. If he shows, I suspect he'll hightail it out of here and wait for a more opportune moment."

"I think so, too." The thought of the attacker simply waiting for a "more opportune moment" didn't sit well with Seth. Mostly because he thought there was a lot of truth in that statement. Until this man was caught, Holly was in danger. Chloe, too.

"Are you armed?" A note of accusation colored Joe's tone.

"Yes."

Montana law didn't require a permit to carry. Anyone who was over eighteen, and eligible to possess a firearm under state law, was allowed to be armed even with a concealed weapon. Seth had never taken advantage of that law until tonight.

Now, while he hoped he didn't have to use his .44 Magnum, he was comforted by its presence. The gun could take down a charging bear. He was confident in its capacity to keep Holly and Chloe safe, if need be.

"Figured you would be," Joe muttered.

He had assumed Joe wouldn't have a lot to say to him, so he was surprised when the man started chatting, reminiscing about the old days.

Seth had been in the cruiser nearly an hour, getting a rundown on what some of his old football teammates had been up to while he'd been enlisted in the military, when a flicker of light in the woods caught his attention.

He interrupted Joe's monologue about the renovation to the football stadium to say, "Did you see that?"

Joe was already reaching for his radio. "I did."

The light flickered again. It was small yet bright. Maybe the flashlight app on a cell phone.

"We've got company," Joe growled. "I didn't think it was likely, but guess I was wrong. I'm calling for backup."

Maybe that was exactly why the attacker had returned. Because he had known it wouldn't be expected.

Seth opened the door and slipped into the night as anger coursed through his veins. Holly didn't deserve this. She and her daughter should be able to rest peacefully in their beds without facing the threat of harm. He would do whatever he could to protect her.

It wasn't the man creeping through the woods that Seth was going after. He would let Joe take care of him as soon as he'd placed his call. It was Holly he was worried about.

The night was inky black, with the moon blanketed by clouds.

Seth used the darkness to his advantage and crept low across the side of the car. The light didn't flicker again. There was no way to know where the intruder had gone.

It was only a moment later when the driver's-side door of the cruiser opened almost soundlessly. He sensed, rather than saw, Officer Joe Rollins creep toward the woods in pursuit of the flickering light. Knowing that Joe had called for backup didn't ease Seth's mind much.

The intruder was here. Now. They didn't have time to wait for help.

While the officer went looking for the attacker, Seth slid his Mag from its holster. Then he moved slowly, stealthily toward the house where Holly and her daughter rested blissfully unaware.

Despite having Chloe nestled in beside her, Holly couldn't stop tossing and turning. Why hadn't she put in a security system? She had thought about it a time or two over the years, but as a single mother, she kept putting off the added expense.

Now, she realized as a single mother, all alone, she should have made it a priority.

She stared blindly at the ceiling in her darkened room, willing sleep to come, yet afraid it would. She didn't want to be caught sleeping and defenseless.

Normally her enormous orange cat, Briar, would be curled up on the bed beside her. The feline's purr always offered comfort. After the chaos tonight, a house full of strangers—officers and medics—she had only spotted the cat briefly as she had darted under Chloe's bed.

She was probably still there, hiding.

Holly didn't blame the cat. Hiding sounded like a pretty good idea. If only she and Chloe had somewhere to go.

A muted and unidentifiable sound made her pop up in bed. It wasn't the first time tonight that something had startled her. Had her house always made so many creaking and groaning noises? How had she never noticed before?

Why didn't she have a gun? It was another safety measure she had considered in the past but put off. It was an expense. Learning to shoot, then practicing the skill seemed like it would take up too much time. Time she didn't have.

That, she realized, was only part of it.

The reason she didn't have a security system, or a weapon, was because she had never really thought she would need them.

It was hard to believe she was in this situation.

There it was again. A sound like she'd never heard before. A *scritching* sort of sound.

She blinked into the darkness, trying to focus.

Scritch-scritch.

That was not the sound of her house settling, not the sound of Briar messing around with something in the dark.

Her stocking feet hit the hardwood floor. It wasn't chilly in her house, but she shivered despite the yoga pants and hoodie she wore. She grabbed the heavy-duty flashlight she had left on her nightstand, then pocketed her cell phone. She was almost dizzy with fear, but she could not give in to that now.

Should she call 911?

That seemed silly. There was already an officer in her driveway.

Was he the cause of the noise?

Surely, if he needed something, he would've just rung the doorbell.

Scritch-scritch.

She hesitated a moment, hating to leave Chloe alone, but she felt she had no choice.

Without turning on any lights, she quickly made her way into the living room so she could peek out the picture window again. She pushed aside the curtain and peered into the yard. It was so dark. She could only vaguely make out the outline of the cruiser in her driveway. She certainly couldn't tell if someone was inside.

She whirled around when she heard the noise again. Her heart felt as if it would explode in her chest. Fear sizzled along her veins, and her breaths turned shallow and raspy.

The sound was coming from her kitchen. Her thoughts flashed to the double French doors that led to the patio. In that moment, she realized the unidentifiable sound was that of something scratching against glass.

Scritch-scritch-scritch.

Someone was trying to break in.

Where was Officer Rollins? Had he fallen asleep? Had he been attacked? Was he hurt? Had her attacker snuck by him, entering her property through the woods in the back? Shuddering, she tried to ignore the terror she felt. She needed to be brave for Chloe.

Tugging her phone from her pocket, she skulked toward the kitchen, straining to make out the peculiar sound. With shaking hands, she dialed.

Her 911 call was answered on the second ring.

"This is Holly Nichols." She kept her tone low, though she didn't think anyone was in the house. Not yet. But she couldn't be sure. "I was attacked earlier tonight. There's an officer stationed in my driveway, Officer Rollins, but I think someone is trying to break into my house. Can you send help?"

"Yes, ma'am." The dispatcher's voice was calm, but Holly was too wired for it to be comforting. "Officer Rollins has already called for backup. They're on their way."

Though that statement should have been reassuring, it sent another frisson of trepidation down Holly's spine because it only affirmed her worst fear.

The attacker was coming for her. Her knees went weak and her hands trembled. Her entire body seemed to tingle with terror. She pressed her back against the wall, pulled in a breath, prayed for strength and calm. Prayed for protection.

Please, watch over Chloe, Lord. Keep her safe from harm. Help me.

Officer Rollins knew someone was here, but where was he?

"Ma'am," the dispatcher said through the line, "are you able to stay on the phone?"

"I don't think so." Holly's tone was breathless and full

of dread. She pushed away from the wall. She didn't have time to fall apart. The threat was coming for her, coming for her child, and she needed to be prepared. "I want my hands free. I won't hang up, but I'm going to slide the phone into my pocket."

She didn't wait for a reply.

Scritch.

The man was trying to enter her house through her kitchen. She had no doubt. While part of her wanted to grab Chloe and hide, her house wasn't that big. There was no place to go where she wouldn't be found sooner rather than later.

Instead, for Chloe's sake, she had to meet her attacker head-on.

As he headed toward Holly's front door, Seth had been stopped by an odd scraping sound coming from the backyard. Though he'd caught sight of the light flickering in the woods again, he was sure the sound coming from the back was the real threat. Using his military training, he'd rushed soundlessly around the back side of the house.

He blinked into the darkness, shocked by what he saw. He had no doubt there was a man in the woods, yet the hulking shape pressed up against the French door was unmistakably a man as well. A man who was trying to gain entry.

Was the man in the woods just a decoy?

Approaching sirens wailed in the distance. There wasn't time to wait for them.

Seth raced forward. In that moment, the man was able to gain entry. He seemed to stumble into the house.

Holly!

He couldn't let the man get to her.

Before he even completed the thought, he heard an angry shout.

A *feminine* shout…followed by a roaring cry of pain.

Seth skidded to a stop in the doorway as light suddenly flooded the kitchen. He blinked against the unexpected brightness and then took in the scene in an instant. A man writhed on the floor. Holly stood next to the light switch, gripping an enormous metal flashlight in her hand.

When she spotted Seth, she reflexively lifted it in the air, ready to swing, then caught herself.

"Seth!" Her dark eyes widened and seemed a stark contrast to her unusually pale face. She pointed at the man who still groaned on the floor. "He…he…" she sputtered, tears and terror clogging her throat.

Seth wanted to go to her, take her in his arms. But now wasn't the time.

The man moved quickly, pushing to his feet. Seth was ready. Gun drawn, he said, "Don't move. I did two stints in the Middle East. I've dealt with worse than a criminal like you."

Blood streamed from the man's crooked nose.

First, he had been pummeled by Chloe's head, now Holly's flashlight. Mother and daughter made a formidable pair.

Without taking his eyes off the intruder, the same man from earlier in the day, he asked Holly, "Do you have something to tie him up with?"

She quickly tugged the thick string out of her hoodie. "Will this work?"

"It's a start."

He explained to the intruder that Holly was going to tie him up. He also explained, in a deadly calm tone, that if the man attempted to hurt Holly in any way, Seth would shoot and have no qualms about it.

The man grumbled and protested but didn't move. Seth got the gist of what he was saying, though he wasn't entirely able to make out his words due to the damage to the man's nose.

Once his hands were firmly tied, Holly jogged off to her room and returned with a belt. The man dropped down onto a kitchen chair. Holly wrapped the belt around his ankles, securing him to the legs of the chair for good measure.

Before she was finished, Officer Rollins entered through the back door.

"What do we have here?" he asked, quickly taking in the broken glass and the tied-up man.

"The real threat," Seth said. "What about the guy in the woods?"

"He got away." Officer Rollins scowled. "But I'm glad to see you got one of them."

"The man in the woods was a decoy?" Seth stated his earlier assumption.

"It seems so. He had quite a head start. He'd flash his light, draw me onward, away from the house, then when we were a good distance off, he went completely dark."

"Wait." Holly threw up a hand as if in protest. "Do you mean there was more than one intruder tonight?" Her eyes darted from Officer Rollins to Seth. She looked frantic. "There's more than one person after me?"

Officer Rollins looked grim. "I think there is just one person after you. Unfortunately, it seems this person has the resources to hire multiple people to get to you." He eyed up the man tied to the chair. "What's your name?"

The man lifted his chin and arched a defiant brow. He said nothing.

"Your friend in the woods got away," Officer Rollins

continued. "Are you going to take the fall for everything that went down tonight?"

Again, no reply.

The officer shrugged. "If you don't feel like talking now, we'll have plenty of time down at the station."

The sirens outside were almost deafening, then they went silent. Vehicle doors slammed.

Backup had arrived and Officer Rollins strode to the front of the house to meet them. Moments later uniformed officers swarmed in. Seth paid them no mind because his attention was completely on Holly. His gaze raked over her, and he determined that while she was rattled, she seemed unharmed.

The intruder was hauled out of the kitchen just as Detective Bianchi walked in.

Seth wanted to offer Holly a hug of reassurance. It wasn't his place, however. Instead, he crossed his arms over his chest and leaned against the kitchen counter, where he would be out of the way.

The detective glanced around, taking in the bloody floor with a bland expression. He turned his attention to Holly.

"What happened?"

Holly pointed at the French door. "He got inside. I don't know how."

Detective Bianchi moved to the door and inspected it. "He used a glass cutter. Cut out a chunk of the pane, then reached in and unlocked it."

Holly nodded slowly, then explained that she heard a noise while she was trying to sleep and got up to investigate.

"When I realized he was coming in, I knew I had to stop him. I stayed close to the wall, hoping he wouldn't be able to see me in the dark." She pointed at the kitchen doorway, then traced the line across the wall where she'd crept to the French door. "I stood there." She pointed at a spot directly next to the door. "When he came in, I swung and hit him square in the face with the flashlight."

Detective Bianchi narrowed his eyes at Seth. "What are you doing here?"

Holly shifted her attention to him as if just now comprehending that he didn't belong. "What *are* you doing here?"

Seth explained how he had ended up in the cruiser. He gave an unapologetic shrug. "After what happened earlier, I couldn't stay away."

"It's a good thing, too," Detective Bianchi said. "Officer Rollins went after the other man, and without you here, Holly might have been left to continue fighting off the intruder. I suspect a broken nose wouldn't have kept him down for long."

Holly seemed to sway and looked ready to fly apart. Seth wanted nothing more than to hold her together. This time, he gave in to his instincts. Pushing away from the counter, he went to her, and she seemed to stumble into his chest.

She was shaking. It was probably his imagination, but he thought he could feel her heart pounding. He could *definitely* hear her ragged breathing.

"It's okay."

"No," she whimpered. "It's not. It's not even a little bit okay."

His arms tightened around her. "It will be."

"You don't know that."

"If you'll excuse me," Detective Bianchi said, "I need to speak with Officer Rollins for a moment."

The two lawmen went outside for some privacy.

Seth stepped away from Holly and placed his hands

on her shoulders. He lowered his head so he could look her in the eye.

Those familiar, deep brown pools held so many emotions. Terror. Misery. Confusion.

His heart ached, knowing how afraid she was in this moment. He could keep telling himself that Holly wasn't his responsibility, that he should just walk away. But the reality of the situation was that he couldn't walk away if he wanted to.

He didn't want to.

He needed to see this through and offer what protection he could.

"You should come home with me." His tone was firm yet somehow pleading. "Come back to Big Sky Ranch."

She started to shake her head.

"I can't…" Seth began, gathered his resolve and then continued, "I can't leave you here. Not like this. Not when someone ran you off the road, tried to kill you, tried to steal your daughter. Now this. I just can't."

"I don't think that's a good idea." She whispered the words as her gaze briefly locked on his, then darted away. "I shouldn't."

"Let's get past the awkwardness. Yes, we have a history. High school was a long time ago." He shrugged. "We need to concentrate on the present. Your life is in danger. Think of your daughter. Someone almost took her tonight. Someone almost killed her mother. What if they try again? Think of Chloe."

Fear flashed across Holly's face, and he knew, in that moment, that her resolve had begun to crumble.

She sighed and glanced over her shoulder, taking in the missing piece of glass in the doorway. Noting the blood splattered across the floor. She shuddered.

"My parents' house recently burned down. It's a long

story for another time. The point is, they're staying with
me while it's being rebuilt. You don't have to worry about
any impropriety." His lip quirked, though he wasn't feeling much humor. "Think of them as chaperones."

"I don't want to put them in danger." She frowned.

He scoffed. "They'd be furious with me if they thought
I left you behind. Trust me, they'd want you somewhere
safe."

Safe.

It was a relative term. While he knew bad things could
still happen at Big Sky Ranch, there was safety in numbers, as the old saying went. He'd feel better knowing his
family was around to help keep an eye on things. They
could offer a modicum of protection.

"Do you have anywhere else to go?" He knew her
mom was long gone, having abandoned her family when
Holly was only eight. And her dad, well, the man was a
jerk on a good day. Absolutely rotten on his worst day.
She had no other family that he was aware of. "A friend
to stay with?"

She shook her head. "I have friends, of course, but
none that I'd feel comfortable going to under the circumstances."

"Dad's good with a rifle. And Mom's a pretty good
shot, too."

Her eyes widened. "Do you think it could come to
that?"

"After what happened here tonight, would you be surprised if it did?" His tone was gentle yet firm. "I'm trying to be realistic."

"You're right." She sighed.

"You're coming with me. You and Chloe." Seth's
tone was decisive. "There have been two attacks on
your home. You are clearly not safe here. You need to

go somewhere they won't think to look for you. I doubt they know who I am. I'm taking you to the ranch. Now."

He knew he sounded bossy. Maybe even arrogant. In that moment, he didn't care. There had been one too many attempts on Holly's life.

"Okay." She nodded as if they both needed the affirmation. "For Chloe's sake, we'll go with you."

Okay? He hadn't expected that, and it only highlighted the fact that she was completely, thoroughly terrified. Rightly so.

"Pack your bags."

"Give me ten minutes."

Seth went outside to let Detective Bianchi know their plan. Then he jogged through the woods to Melanie's parents to retrieve his truck. By the time he returned Holly was standing in the entryway. Two bags were packed at her feet, and her sleeping daughter was nestled in her arms.

She looked vulnerable. Her face bruised, her hair in disarray.

She was still beautiful.

"Ready?"

Looking hesitant, Holly nodded. Seth couldn't help but wonder if she was as baffled by the day's turn of events as he was.

What had he gotten himself—and his battered heart—into?

FOUR

It felt more than a little surreal to be sitting in her high school sweetheart's kitchen along with his parents and her daughter, eating bunny-shaped pancakes drowning in syrup. All the while, Chloe was regaling Seth and his parents, James and Julia, with stories of her weekend swimming lessons.

Holly had feared that Chloe would be fretful after nearly being kidnapped. But children were resilient, and she was easily distracted by the horses and cattle in the pasture.

The pancakes, whipped up by Julia at Chloe's request, had also been a good distraction.

While Chloe may have forgotten about last night, Holly could not. She ate her breakfast so as not to draw attention to herself. Her nerves were so raw, so frazzled her stomach churned with every bite. It was surprising that she'd gotten any sleep last night. Yet, sleeping in Seth's den on his futon with Chloe, she had felt relatively safe, and had managed to doze off.

Safe, because she knew Seth's top-notch security alarm was set, and he and his father had taken turns keeping watch.

She had learned that Seth's parents' house, which was

located on the other side of the property, had burned due to an act of arson in spring earlier this year. Because of this, there had been quite the battle with their insurance company. Then there had been one delay after another. What was supposed to have been a short stay as their house was rebuilt had turned into nearly half a year. However, Seth had commented that the house was nearing completion, so there was an end in sight.

Holly wasn't happy to hear about their dilemma, but she was grateful for their presence.

"Can I?" Chloe asked.

Holly knew, by her tone, that it was not the first time Chloe asked. She had missed her daughter's question. Her little girl stared at her hopefully.

"I'm sorry. What would you like?" Holly's gaze skipped around the table, and she realized all eyes were on her. She was embarrassed at having been caught not paying attention.

"Chloe was asking if she could go see the horses," Julia patiently explained.

Holly's gaze darted to Chloe, who nodded and grinned. "Is it okay? The cows are away in another pasture. But the horses are right out front."

Holly caught Seth's eye. He gave her a subtle, encouraging nod. While she'd like nothing more than to hover by Chloe's side until this whole ordeal was behind them, she knew it wasn't in Chloe's best interest to smother her that way.

"James and I will both go with her," Julia encouraged. "We won't let her out of our sight."

"Yes, that would be all right." Holly forced a smile. "I'd appreciate that."

"Yay!" Chloe's little fist pumped in the air, a gesture she'd learned from her babysitter. She slid her chair back.

"Hold up. You need to wait for everyone to finish eating."

"We are finished, Mom." Chloe looked at Holly's plate. "Well, not you. But everyone else."

Holly glanced around again. Sure enough, everyone else was done eating. She hadn't realized how much her mind had been wandering. She needed to pull herself together.

"I saw her outdoor gear in the entryway." Julia gave Holly a gentle, understanding smile. "I'll get her ready. You enjoy your coffee."

"Thank you."

She watched her daughter leave the kitchen with Seth's parents. Chloe was chattering away, and they seemed to be enjoying every word.

When Holly swung her attention back to Seth, she realized he was studying her.

"How are you this morning?"

Her heart lurched. After a decade, Seth looked the same. Yet different.

He was taller, broader. Tougher. She thought joining the military probably had something to do with that. However, he was as handsome as ever, with his neatly cut dark hair, deep blue eyes and chiseled cheekbones that had made her swoon as a teenager.

"I'm okay." She was irritated with herself for nearly swooning now. Because one thing about him that hadn't changed, apparently, was his ability to take her breath away. "I'm worried about Melanie. I hope she's not traumatized after what happened."

"I saw her briefly when I spoke to her parents last night, getting permission to park on their driveway." Seth's tone was calming. "They seem very protective. Very supportive. I'm sure she'll be all right. She was worried about you and Chloe, though. She asked how you were doing."

Holly smiled. "Mel's a good kid."

"She's very fond of your daughter. Does she watch her a lot?"

Holly was grateful for the easy conversation. She nodded.

"Melanie has been babysitting Chloe every Wednesday night for nearly half a year. She's fifteen, saving for a car. One evening last spring she knocked on my door and asked if I was interested in hiring her for odd jobs." Holly smiled. "She was working her way through our neighborhood. She had started mowing the lawn for the Thompsons, cleaning for Mrs. Crenshaw and cooking meals two nights a week for Mr. Wheaton, who was widowed last year. I thought about it a bit and decided I could use some *me* time. So every Wednesday night, I go for a bike ride. If the weather is bad, I join a yoga class in town. It gives me time to mentally decompress, and it puts a bit of money in Mel's bank account."

"She's an industrious girl."

A vision of Melanie pounding against the attacker's back flittered through Holly's mind. "And so brave."

"Is Chloe missing school?" Seth asked.

"She is." Holly winced, hating the negative impact on her daughter. "I spoke with her teacher this morning. She promised to help Chloe catch up on anything she misses."

She reached for her coffee, but before she could bring it to her lips, her phone buzzed. She didn't typically bring her phone to the table, but today was not typical. Since her phone had been lost in the river, she had dug out her old, battered phone that had seen better days and had reactivated it. When she got a chance, she'd get a new one. For now, the old one would do.

"It's Mateo."

Seth motioned for her to answer.

"Hi, Mateo. I'm with Seth. Is it okay if I put you on speakerphone?" She knew she would end up relaying everything to Seth anyway. This would save time.

"It's okay by me."

The detective was matter-of-fact as he gave her an update: the man who broke into her home last night wasn't saying a word. Literally. Not a word.

"Do you know who the guy is?" Seth asked.

"Career criminal by the name of Barry Ellis. He has a rap sheet as long as my arm, but most recently, he'd been serving time on assault charges. Was released less than two weeks ago."

"Has he lawyered up?"

"He hasn't. When asked, he just gives us a sullen glare. I suppose he doesn't want to talk to a lawyer, either. That tactic isn't going to get him very far." The detective cleared his throat. "That's only part of the reason I'm calling."

Holly met Seth's eyes across the table.

"What's the other reason?" she asked.

"Since this man isn't talking, and I have a hunch he won't, we don't have much to go on. Would you consider going through with meeting the woman in the park?"

"No," Seth said before Holly could answer.

She shot him an irritated look.

The phone call she'd received yesterday could be a lead. It could be their *only* lead.

"It's not a good idea." Seth frowned. "It's too dangerous."

"I would never put Holly, or anyone, in danger." The detective sounded insulted at the suggestion. "We'd canvas the area. Fill the park with plainclothes officers. I'd be right there."

"I don't like it."

Holly didn't like it, either, but what choice did she have? If this could lead to whoever was after her, she needed to go through with it. As Mateo said, they had no other leads. What if this was their only chance to find out who wanted her dead?

What if she turned him down and someone ended up getting to Chloe? She would never forgive herself for not trying to get information when she had the chance.

A shiver trickled down her spine. She made her decision. "I'll do it."

Seth let out a huff and slumped against his chair.

"Thanks, Holly. You said the meeting was supposed to be at eleven today. That's a little less than three hours from now," Mateo noted. "I'm going to get everything set up. I'll call you back with the details of where you need to be and when so we can get you wired up."

It was a beautiful autumn day. The perfect sort of day to enjoy a stroll through the park. It was *not* a good day to use Holly as a decoy. There would never be a good day for that. Seth knew she wasn't really being used as a decoy, yet to him it felt like it. He knew the detective was hoping the caller would show up and give Holly some much-needed information.

Seth leaned against the metal railing that ran along the river, the same river that had saved Holly the night before. The flowing water was shed from a distant mountain and snaked through towns and wilderness. He tried to look nonchalant. Just a guy, enjoying some afternoon sunshine.

He pulled out his phone and pretended to text while

watching Holly behind his aviator sunglasses. She looked classy in her fuchsia peacoat and knee-high, black boots. She had told the caller she would be wearing the coat as a way to be identified. Her dark hair was pulled back in a sleek ponytail to keep it from whipping around in the wind. She sat on the bench, the one by the duck pond, right where she'd told the caller she would be.

Seth glanced around, knowing the park was full of officers that had been called in just for this. Mateo hadn't wanted Seth to be involved. But there was no way that he was going to stay behind with Chloe and his parents.

No. Way.

So here he was.

Mateo jogged up to him, wearing running pants, a windbreaker and a baseball cap. He wasn't used to seeing the detective look so casual. Must be the guy's idea of dressing for undercover work.

He was sure the lawman's lightweight jacket was hiding his weapon. Seth's own weapon rested reassuringly against his side, also covered by his coat, but easily accessible.

"Hey, Detective." Seth nodded in greeting. "Have you got anything yet?"

"You know, Seth, after working your brother's case, and now this one, I feel like we should be on a first-name basis. Call me Mateo."

"Sure thing."

"To answer your question, I've got eyes on the parking lot and every entrance of the park. My people haven't seen anyone they suspect could be the caller." Mateo twisted around, leaning up against the railing next to Seth.

He, too, hid behind his sunglasses.

Seth was acutely aware of Holly leaning back on the

bench. He knew she was trying to look relaxed, but to him, she looked ready to bolt. She toyed with her ponytail, then glanced over her shoulder, clearly scoping out the park.

He did the same as he wished he could sit beside her. Obviously, that wouldn't do. He had to keep his distance, whether he liked it or not.

"It's eleven," he said after a quick glance at his phone.

"If the caller heard about the attack last night, I'm afraid they'll be a no-show. But we had to try."

"Mateo, I feel like she's just sitting there with a target on her back."

"She's not." Mateo's tone was firm. "The department has people all around the perimeter of the park. We started checking the place out the minute I got off the phone with Holly hours ago." He pushed away from the railing. Seth knew he didn't want to linger too long. "See you in a bit."

Mateo took off at a jog, following the trail that looped the park in a way that would keep Holly in his sight.

Seth wished he'd thought to dress in running gear. He'd look a bit foolish jogging around the park in cowboy boots, jeans and his lined denim jacket.

Instead, he sauntered over to a nearby bench and took a seat. He tossed an arm across the back of the bench, a completely relaxed pose, and pretended to take a phone call. Really, the gash in his side had begun to throb. Stretching out helped him relax the muscles involved.

Stupid knife wound.

He'd do it all again in a heartbeat since it had meant getting Chloe and Holly away from the attacker.

The next half hour was excruciating.

Holly continued to pretend to play on her phone.

Mateo kept up with his slow jog.

Seth stayed on his nonexistent call.

Finally, a car alarm sounded briefly from the side street. It was the signal that they were giving up for the day. He couldn't help but feel disappointed. It was as if they had put Holly at risk for nothing. At least she was unharmed.

Seth watched as she stood and casually stretched. Then she headed toward the parking lot.

Seth waited only a moment before sliding from his bench as well. He scanned the area as he strode toward his vehicle. Holly, who had gotten there first and who had his extra set of keys, was already inside.

Mateo was across the parking lot and Seth gave him a subtle nod. Since the caller didn't show, the plan was to meet up at the police station.

He hopped in his truck and glanced at Holly, who was clearly distraught.

"I don't understand why she didn't show up." Her gaze darted around the park as if she still held out hope. "She was so determined yesterday."

"It's possible she heard about your attack," Seth suggested. "Everyone in your neighborhood knew about it, and news travels fast."

She pinched the bridge of her nose.

"I know. I was hoping that if she didn't show, she'd at least call." She stared at the phone in her hand, as if willing it to ring.

It didn't.

Seth pulled out of the lot, scanning for trouble, as was the habit instilled in him. They rolled out onto the quiet street lined with residential homes.

"At least you tried. There's nothing else you could have done."

"I know, Seth. Still—"

"Down!" The command flew from his mouth the split instant he saw a man step around an enormous oak tree.

The windshield shattered as a bullet tore through the truck. Seth felt as though his heart had been ripped right out of his chest.

"Holly!" A million unspoken pleas and prayers flew through his mind in that moment in time. He twisted the wheel, sending the truck sideways, putting himself between Holly and any more oncoming bullets. He was vaguely aware of the back seat window shattering as another bullet ripped through his vehicle.

"Holly," he said frantically, "are you hurt?"

"I'm okay!" Her voice was breathless. Shocked. Quaking.

She was nearly crouched into a ball beside him, having ducked the instant he'd issued the command. She peered up at him, her eyes once again full of terror.

Sirens, likely the unmarked police cars that were nearby, began to wail. When Seth looked for the shooter, he didn't see him. He'd likely taken off, racing through the maze of homes. But Seth didn't know that for sure.

Part of him wanted to draw his weapon and chase after the man. He wanted to hunt him down the way these men had been hunting Holly down. Yet he couldn't, absolutely wouldn't, leave Holly alone.

She shifted.

"Please stay down," he urged. "I'm not sure it's safe yet."

He swerved in the street, jostled over a curb then whipped the truck down a side street he hadn't planned on taking. Glancing over again, he realized the bullet had torn through the passenger seat. If Holly hadn't crouched the moment he'd said to, the bullet would've torn right through her chest.

His own chest tightened at the thought, and his heart beat wildly.

Thank You, Jesus. He silently repeated the words over and over as he put distance between them and the shooter. He could say them a million times, and they wouldn't be enough.

When he cruised into the police station parking lot, Mateo, gun drawn and eyes darting all around, jogged across the pavement to greet them. Other armed officers filled the lot.

Even here, at the police station and under protection, he didn't feel safe.

As Holly slowly sat up, then spotted the bullet hole that ripped through her seat, he wondered if she would ever feel safe again.

Sitting in an interview room across from Mateo, Holly felt as if her heart rate was never going to slow. She had almost been killed again. If Seth hadn't seen the man—

No. It did no good to entertain that thought.

She turned her attention to Seth, who was glaring at Mateo.

"You said you had the park covered," Seth growled.

"I did have the park covered." Mateo's tone was calm, firm. "You weren't in the park. It's not like I can have the whole town covered."

"But that was close to the park," Seth argued.

She reached over and put a hand on Seth's. He startled at her touch. When he turned to face her, she realized he wasn't angry. Not really. He was scared. Scared because she'd almost been shot.

"It's not Mateo's fault." Her voice was calming when she squeezed his hand. "I was at the park for half an hour and I was safe. He's right. It's not possible to cover the whole town."

Seth seemed to deflate some and scraped his free hand over his face. "I know. I'm just…" He seemed to flounder for the word frustrated.

"It's a rotten situation all around," Mateo agreed.

Holly knew Seth was irritated with himself as well. When asked for a description, he hadn't been able to give them much to go on. The shooter was medium height, stocky, but had been wearing a skullcap and sunglasses, which obscured any identifying features. That was more than Holly had been able to give. She hadn't seen the shooter at all.

When Seth had yelled for her to get down, she'd simply acted on his demand.

His warning had, undoubtedly, saved her life.

"Where do we go from here?"

"Our perp still hasn't uttered a word." Mateo referenced the man who had broken into her house. "But we're digging into his background, trying to see who he's been in contact with lately. We had a search warrant for his place, a trailer in a park on the edge of town. That didn't turn up anything. The department is still searching for the other man, the one who acted as decoy. I suspect that man is the same guy who shot at you today."

"I know you're good at your job. I know you'll figure out who is behind this."

Would he figure it out soon enough, though? Holly couldn't let that fear take hold.

"Any chance you could leave town for a while?" Mateo asked.

"I don't like that idea," Seth interjected.

Holly swung her gaze to him.

"I don't." His tone was unapologetic, but his eyes were

pleading. "What if they follow you? There's no guarantee they won't. You can stay at the ranch. I have a good security system. My brother, Eric, and his wife, Cassie, are nearby. They can help keep an eye out."

Holly bit her lip. She was more tempted by his offer than she wanted to admit. But should she?

"Where would you go?" Seth demanded when she hesitated. "Some hotel somewhere? You'd constantly be looking over your shoulder."

"Do you have any family you could stay with?" Mateo asked.

"No." Her father was her only living blood relative. They were not close despite Holly's efforts over the last few years to build a relationship with him. He was the reason she'd returned to Mulberry Creek after earning her degree, but she may as well have stayed away. He wanted nothing to do with her and she'd come to accept that. "There's no one."

"I could find a place for you to lie low."

Seth shot Mateo a look.

Mateo shrugged. "It's just an offer. I know more than one person who has a cabin—"

"I'd have to go with," Seth said.

Holly held up her hand. "I'd rather not go anywhere."

Seth's relief was obvious. It was hard not to wonder why he was so adamant. Must be his innately protective nature coming out.

"If you really don't mind us staying at the ranch, despite the danger, I think it's the best place for Chloe. She already adores your parents, and I think she's comfortable there." The truth was, Seth's parents had greeted her last night as if there wasn't a decade of disconnect between them. She craved and appreciated the support of family more than she wanted to admit. "To be honest, with your security system and people around, I felt safe there."

"I don't mind."

Holly's relic of a phone chimed. The sound was muffled because it rested in the depths of her purse. She pulled it out and glanced at it, then looked up and realized both men were looking at her expectantly.

She held her phone out for them to see. It was old, battered and had a cracked screen. Yet the message came through just fine.

A text.

From an anonymous number.

I'm sorry I put you in danger. It's not safe to meet. Read the file I sent. I wish it could be more.

Seth glanced at Holly, then Mateo, then back at Holly.

"What file?" he demanded.

"Sent where?" Mateo wondered, his tone stark with frustration. "Your home? Your office? Your email? Sent courier? Postal service? Electronically?"

She shook her head, as baffled as the men. "I wish I knew."

"We'll need your phone," Mateo said. "I doubt the call is traceable, but we need to try."

"*I* need my phone." Holly frowned. "I can't be without it, Mateo. I'm a CASA volunteer."

"A what?" Seth asked.

"Court Appointed Special Advocate," Holly explained. "I work with teen girls in the foster care system. The girl I'm working with now has a court case coming up soon. I need to be able to reach her. More importantly, she needs to be able to reach me. As the title implies, I advocate for the child. I take my role very seriously."

"You can give her my number just until we can get you a new phone," Seth suggested.

When would that be? It wasn't like they were going to sashay into the nearest store when she had people shooting at her. Yet she knew it was futile to argue. Mateo was right. They needed her phone. This was an active investigation. She couldn't really say no, so she placed it on the table and slid it his way.

"Does this mean that the attacks on me have to do with the woman who called yesterday?"

"I can't say for sure, though it certainly seems likely. Anything else you can think of to share?" Mateo waited a beat, but neither spoke up. "If not, one of the officers can give you a ride home."

"We've got a ride." Seth frowned. "I knew you'd have to keep my truck for the ballistics report. My dad should be here any minute."

"All right, then." Mateo grabbed Holly's phone and got to his feet. "I'll keep in touch. Meanwhile, you two stay safe."

Stay safe.

Such simple words.

Such a daunting task.

FIVE

Seth had been expecting his dad to pick them up at the police station. When he saw his brother Eric's truck pull up right to the front door—so he and Holly wouldn't be exposed walking across the parking lot—he was more than a little surprised.

Was it only yesterday that he and Eric had it out? It seemed like a lifetime ago.

He opened the back door of the double cab truck for Holly. As soon as she was settled in, he hopped into the passenger seat.

"Where's Dad?" Seth wondered.

"Hello to you, too. Dad's busy playing with the kiddos. Wyatt wanted to meet Chloe." Eric's tone softened as he spoke of his son, whom he'd only recently discovered. "We brought over a tote of toys. Now Dad and the kids have a replica of the ranch set up in your living room."

"Oh." Their dad loved kids, so this really wasn't a surprise.

"Hi, Holly." Eric glanced over his shoulder and gave her a friendly nod. "I wish the circumstances were better, but it's good to see you again after all these years. Your daughter is adorable."

A smile flickered across her face. "Thank you. It's good to see you as well. I look forward to meeting Wyatt."

Eric pulled out of the lot as Seth kept watch for any sign of trouble.

"You'll get a chance to meet him," Eric said. "Are you sticking around at the ranch for a while?"

"Yes. I hope that's okay. As you mentioned, the circumstances are hardly ideal. I don't want to put anyone in danger. I would understand if you don't want me around."

"Don't worry about us." Eric caught her eye in the rearview mirror and gave a reassuring smile. "We can take care of ourselves. It's you and Chloe who need protection. We're happy to help provide that."

His words brought Seth a sense of relief. Really, he probably should've discussed the matter with Eric and Cassie. They lived on the other side of the ranch. Far enough away for complete privacy, but close enough that—worst-case scenario—they could be in the line of danger if the situation with Holly got any more heated. However, the events of the past twenty-four hours had happened so fast it wasn't as if he'd had a chance.

Eric went on. "As long as you're sticking around, maybe you could try to talk some sense into Seth."

Irritation immediately sizzled down Seth's spine because he knew exactly what his brother was doing.

"Eric." His voice held a warning tone as yesterday's argument whirled through his mind. "Now is not the time."

In true big-brother fashion, Eric completely ignored Seth's attempt to get him to drop the subject.

"You see, Seth thinks he's going to quit ranching." Eric's tone was deceptively conversational, but Seth could hear the edge of irritation that lay beneath the surface. "He wants me to buy out his half of the ranch. Has big plans to move to Bozeman and join his friend Tucker's extreme-adventure business. He's even trying to get our sister, Nina, to buy his house now that she's moved back to town and is renting a place."

Seth couldn't stop himself from glancing over his shoulder at Holly. He wondered if she could hear the annoyance in Eric's voice. They'd had a doozy of an argument over this yesterday afternoon. Bad enough that Seth had stormed out of the house, hopped into his truck for a calming drive and stumbled upon Holly instead.

Eric was clearly still mad.

No surprise there. He thought Seth was being rash, impulsive and childish for wanting to partner in an adventure company. In truth, Seth just wanted something... more. His life had started to feel empty. He hoped that guided white water rafting tours and extended mountain hikes would help cure that. Eric hadn't wanted to hear it. His big brother had accused him of bailing on the family business.

Which, he supposed, was technically accurate. Even if it was a bit unfair to put it that way.

Holly said nothing as she blinked those big, beautiful brown eyes at him in surprise.

"Tucker's uncle is retiring," Eric continued on, "and he invited Seth to buy out his uncle's half."

"An extreme-adventure business in Bozeman," Holly echoed. "That'll be quite the change."

The plan that he'd been working on for months, the one he'd finally admitted to Eric, had sounded so good in his head. Somehow, hearing it come from Holly, it didn't sound so great. The plan was already set in motion. He and Tucker had been tossing the idea around for nearly a year, from the time Tucker's uncle had first contemplated retirement.

"Says he needs a change," Eric continued to tattle.

Yes, Seth could definitely hear the veiled anger in his brother's tone and figured Holly could, too.

"How soon are you leaving?"

He glanced at her again. She flashed him a smile. Was it forced? There certainly was none of her usual sparkle behind it.

"Six months." Eric blurted the words before Seth could answer. "He's taking off in six months. Sooner if he can arrange it. Can you believe that? Just up and walking away from his life here to go look for adventure."

"That's enough about me." Seth was not happy about having his life plans scrutinized. He turned his attention to Eric. "Did Dad fill you in on everything that happened last night?"

"He did." Eric easily accepted the topic change. "I take it today didn't go well, either."

"It didn't." Relieved to have the attention off his impending move, he told Eric what had gone down at the park and after.

Eric let out a low whistle. "You were shot at right in town? Whoever this is, they mean business. I was wondering how you ended up without a vehicle. I wasn't expecting that."

"Um, guys?" Holly chimed in from the back seat. "Could I ask a favor?"

"Of course." Seth twisted around to look at her again. "What do you need?"

"Could we stop by my house?" She winced and her tone was apologetic, as if she really hated to ask for anything. "We could get my vehicle."

Seth was about to tell her no, it wasn't worth the risk, but she continued.

"Also, I really need to check on Briar." Holly's concern was evident. "I'm sure she's out of food."

"Briar?" Seth asked.

"My cat. I filled her bowl before we left last night, but she's not one to ration," Holly explained. "I imagine she ate two days' worth in one sitting and now thinks she's starving."

Seth exchanged a glance with Eric.

Eric shrugged. "It's your call. But isn't it still a crime scene?"

"Mateo said they wrapped up everything last night." Holly shifted in her seat. "We don't have to worry about that."

"We'll stop as long as we make it quick." He didn't think it was the best idea. However, he was not the type of guy who wanted to see a cat starve. Besides, if they picked up Holly's vehicle, he wouldn't have to endure any more of this truck ride with his traitorous, blabbermouth brother.

Seth was leaving. It was all Holly could think of as they pulled up in front of her house. She had finally run into him again after all these years, only to find out that he wasn't staying. There was no reason to feel the sense of loss that had drifted over her. Seth was her friend, and barely that. He had every right to do whatever he chose with his life.

The gentle breeze flitted through her hair as she and Seth hustled up her short sidewalk. Holly couldn't get Eric's words out of her mind as she fumbled with the lock on her front door. There was no reason in the world for that knowledge to bother her.

Yet it did.

"Hey, you can wait in the truck with Eric." Seth misinterpreted the tremble in her hands for fear. "I can take care of things inside."

She was upset, yes. But she wasn't afraid. At least, not any more afraid than she'd been for the better part of the day. She was…disappointed, maybe even sad, if truth be told. She didn't want Seth to leave town. That was silly because she had absolutely no right to want him to stay.

She looked over her shoulder at him and forced a smile. "I'm fine. Let's get in and get out."

The door swung open, and they traipsed inside. Holly stopped in the entryway as Seth closed the door behind them.

Something wasn't right. She glanced around her home, the place that had been a sanctuary for herself and Chloe. A chill trickled down her spine. From the entryway she could see into her cozy living room. A small stack of children's board books and a rumpled lap blanket rested on the sofa. A few toys were scattered on the floor. The room looked comfortably lived in, as it always had.

Yet something was off.

It took only a second for her to realize what was not right.

She turned to Seth and pressed a finger to his lips, a silent warning for him to be quiet. Then she pointed at Briar, her enormous apricot-colored, long-haired, fluffy-tailed cat.

Seth's eyes widened in understanding.

The hefty feline was pacing back and forth in front of the closet door. Tail twitching, amber eyes shining indignantly. Something—or likely someone—had invaded the cat's space.

Holly did not think it was something as innocuous as a mouse.

"You go feed the cat." Seth's tone was smooth. However, the look he gave her held an edge of warning. "I'll back your car out of the garage. I'd like to get out of here as soon as possible. No sense in lingering."

Even as he said the words, he drew his weapon.

"Sure thing. Let's make this quick." Holly played along, pretending nothing was amiss and that they were going about their business. Was her voice shaking? She hoped not, yet feared it was.

Seth pointed at the closet door, indicating she should open it, and then shield herself behind it. He took a step back, gun aimed, ready to fire. She reached for the door-knob. When he nodded, she turned the knob, tugged the closet door open—

"Hey," Eric said as he let himself in the front door, startling them all. "I—"

A man flew out of the closet, the hood of his sweat-shirt wrapped loosely around his face, the strings tied so he had a large peephole to see through. He swung Holly's laptop at Seth's head.

Seth, who had been distracted by the unexpected ap-pearance of his brother, didn't have time to do anything more than duck. The laptop, not connecting with Seth, whipped around and smashed into pieces against the wall.

The man grabbed Holly and flung her at Seth. She crashed into him, and he groaned as her elbow jabbed his day-old knife wound. In the moment it took for them to steady themselves, the intruder darted toward the back of the house.

The entire ordeal lasted a matter of seconds.

Eric lunged forward as he realized what was happen-ing. Seth shoved Holly into his arms.

"Watch her!" he shouted.

Then he raced after the man.

Holly's heart pounded so frantically in her chest that

it ached. She immediately disentangled herself from Eric and raced off the way Seth had gone.

"Don't go after him," Eric ordered.

Holly entered the kitchen and went straight to the counter. She pulled a long, sharp knife from her butcher block.

"I'm not going after Seth. However, I'm going to be prepared if that man comes back." She glanced around. "Or if, like last night, he wasn't alone."

"Good idea." Eric chose a knife for himself. He strode toward the door. Holly could tell he wanted to chase after his brother. Seth had pursued the man into the woods. It was impossible to know which direction they'd gone.

"I'm calling 911." Eric pulled his phone out of his pocket. In no time, he had connected with emergency dispatch.

Clutching her weapon, Holly glanced around her kitchen, a room that she used to find so warm and inviting. Now it felt sinister and foreign. How many loaves of whole wheat bread had she and Chloe made in here? How many pots of soup, batches of cookies? How many crafts had they created at that table? Her kitchen had been a room full of love and joy as she had bonded with her new daughter.

Now all she could see were the remnants of blood staining the floor after the ordeal last night. Today's intruder had busted out the pane that someone on the department had boarded up. Twice now, it had been the place of entry for someone who apparently wanted her dead.

It was such a horrific thought it took her breath away.

"I need to install a security system," she muttered as she went to the door.

Where was Seth? Her hands trembled and she fought

down the fear his absence elicited. If something happened to him… She could barely stand the thought. And if something bad happened to him because of her, she didn't think she would ever get over it. The wound he'd sustained last night was already almost more than she could bear.

It felt like forever since he'd darted out of the house, though she knew it had only been a matter of minutes. Her gaze scanned the tree line.

Please Lord, I know I've asked for a lot over these past two days, but I'm asking once again that You keep Seth safe.

"A security system is not a bad idea," Eric said.

Her mind was no longer on the security system.

"Come on, Seth. Where are you?" she murmured.

Eric reached over and patted her shoulder reassuringly. "He's fine. He can handle this."

Something about his tone made Holly think he said the words to reassure himself as much as to reassure her.

Silently begging God for Seth's safety over and over again, she stared into the woods.

She hated standing here. But what else could she do? Run blindly after Seth and their attacker? That would only complicate matters.

After what felt like an eternity, Seth strode out of the trees and into the yard.

Holly exhaled an enormous breath of relief.

Instead of waiting for him, she darted out the door and across the lawn. She was so relieved to see him she hugged him tight without thought. "You're okay! I was so worried."

He groaned, the sound holding a bit of agony, and she immediately stepped back.

"You were fine," she said with a wince, "before I

crushed your wound. Again. I'm sorry." She moved away and wrapped her arms around her stomach, lest she get the silly notion to wrap herself around him again.

"No need to apologize." He took her by the arm and they hurried back to the house. "Let's get you inside."

He cocked his head as if trying to make out a distant sound.

"Sirens," Holly clarified. "Eric called for help."

Within moments two cruisers pulled up. Eric waved them in from the front steps. The officers came inside, made sure the area was clear, then asked Holly to determine if anything other than her laptop had been tampered with.

One of the officers bagged up the busted laptop, hoping to get prints off it.

As far as Holly could tell, nothing else had been stolen. Though now that she was scanning her house with a critical eye, she could see that a few drawers had been left slightly open. The clothes in her closet weren't hanging as precisely as she'd left them. The mattress on Chloe's bed was ever so slightly askew, as if someone had been searching for something underneath it.

She shuddered as a sick feeling washed over her. Knowing her home had been breached twice sent fear arrowing into her bones. How was she ever going to stay here again?

What had they been looking for? The elusive files from the unknown woman?

Seth had told the officers that the man could have been the man who shot at Holly the day before. They were both on the shorter side with a wiry build. But yesterday he had only glimpsed the man's face, and today none of them had been able to make out his face at all.

Seth put a hand on her shoulder. "Are you okay?"

Holly wanted nothing more than to lean into him again. She needed to stop relying on him so much. For her own sake, she had to be strong. She drew in a breath and blew it out, trying to calm her frazzled nerves. "Yes."

He gave her a steady, disbelieving look.

"Okay, not really." No sense trying to fake it since he knew the truth already. "I'm not okay. But I will be."

He nodded, accepting that answer, and gave her a quick, friendly side hug.

"Holly, I have a few more questions, then you're free to go," Lainie Hughes said. She was the officer who had sat with Chloe at the hospital while Mateo questioned them last night. Holly found the woman to be caring yet efficient. Both were qualities she appreciated.

"Sure."

"I'll let you wrap up here. I'll get Briar loaded up and get your car out of the garage."

"Briar?" Holly was surprised and more than a little relieved when she understood what Seth was suggesting. "We're taking her with us?"

"We can't leave her here." Seth shrugged, as if that should be obvious. "We owe her for her excellent sentry duties. That guy could've ambushed us if she hadn't warned us he was here. Besides, I'm sure Chloe will be happy to see her. I'll round Briar up and gather her supplies. I spotted them in the laundry room when we were looking around for things out of place."

Holly nodded, once again grateful for Seth's presence, for his thoughtfulness. Yes, Chloe would be delighted. It was so very considerate of Seth to think of both her daughter and her cat.

She was even more grateful for the fact that he was about to get her out of here.

* * *

"That was a reckless move." Eric's tone was scolding as he placed a bag of cat food in the back seat of Holly's sensible silver Prius. "You shouldn't have chased after that guy."

Seth, having settled a grumpy Briar, cat carrier and all, in the back of the vehicle, closed the hatchback and turned to his brother. He was thankful for the relative privacy of Holly's garage.

"We'd have the guy in custody if you had stayed in the truck," Seth shot back. "If you hadn't barged in, I would've apprehended him."

"What? You're law enforcement now?" Eric demanded. "Trying to make a citizen's arrest?"

Seth shook his head. "Why do you always have to second-guess me? What do you think I did when I was in the Marines? Do you think I just sat in the barracks eating chocolate chip cookies Mom sent while playing Go Fish?"

Eric had the decency to look embarrassed. "No."

"I put my life on the line for my country. I went after bad guys. It's what I was trained to do. I've been in war zones with artillery fire and bombs going off." He wasn't glib enough to say chasing a man through the woods as he'd done today, one on one, was child's play. However, it was certainly not nearly as harrowing as other situations he'd been in. "So yeah, when a guy breaks into Holly's house, I'm going to go after him, too." He paused and looked imploringly at his brother. "I'd appreciate it if you didn't talk down to me for it."

Eric looked genuinely startled. "I don't talk down to you."

Seth arched a brow.

Eric scrubbed a hand over his face as realization settled in. "I'm sorry. I sure didn't mean to. It's just that I feel protective. Especially after losing Ella. You may be a big, tough soldier, but you're still my baby brother." He clapped a hand on Seth's shoulder. "I'm sorry. I guess, to be honest, I'm still on edge after we argued yesterday. I don't like fighting with you. Telling me you were leaving the ranch hit me out of the clear blue. I wish you wouldn't make such a hasty decision."

"It's not hasty," Seth assured him. "I've thought it over for months. Going into business with Tucker is what I want to do. It's the right decision for me. It's not fair for you to try to talk me out of it."

"I guess when you're used to all the action and excitement you had in the military, ranch life must be monotonous."

"It's not that." Seth didn't know how to explain his reasoning, yet knew he owed it to Eric to try. "I feel like something is missing. I need to try something different."

"And partnering with Tucker is it." Eric sounded resigned.

"Yeah."

But was it?

Glancing up, he saw Holly standing in the doorway that separated the garage from the house. She clutched a small, pink knitted blanket to her chest. She looked rattled, still, and he couldn't blame her.

"Are you finished inside?" Seth asked.

"We are." Her gaze bounced between the brothers. She frowned. "I didn't mean to interrupt."

Seth inwardly cringed, wondering how much of the conversation Holly had heard. Not that it mattered, as Eric had already told her more than she needed to know on the drive here.

Eric waved her off. "You didn't. This conversation is over. Seth is starting a new life soon, and that's that."

Seth hoped his brother had finally, begrudgingly, accepted his decision. Or maybe he was simply letting it go for the time being. Regardless, it was time for a change in topic. Discussing his move in front of Holly made him uncomfortable, though it shouldn't.

"What did you come in the house for?" Seth wondered why his brother had come storming in, disrupting them as they were about to apprehend the intruder. "I thought you were going to wait in your truck."

"Oh, right. Cassie texted to say that Chloe was asking for her blanket. She asked me to let you know. I assume she has a special one."

Holly nodded as she lifted the knitted blanket she held into the air. "She does. This is it. I didn't think to grab it last night, and she was already missing it."

"Do you have everything you need?" Eric asked.

Holly glanced at Seth. "I think so."

"Briar is loaded up," Seth assured her.

A small smile flitted across Holly's lips, letting Seth know he'd made the right call in insisting the cat come to the ranch. He wasn't a cat lover. They were such persnickety creatures. However, he did not like the idea of an intruder coming back yet again. This way, they would all know the fluffy feline was safe.

"Officer Hughes said she'd escort us back to the ranch," Holly said.

"Perfect. Then I'm going to run an errand. I'll see you two later." Eric tapped the garage door opener, and once it lifted he strode toward his truck.

Seth could hear Briar loudly complaining from inside the car.

"I suspect she's not crazy about the cat carrier."

"Not even a little," Holly agreed.

"Then are you ready to get out of here?"

A small shudder rippled through her. "Yes, Seth. Please take me to my daughter."

He motioned toward her car, opening the passenger door for her. Once she was safely inside, he glanced around, wondering if the attacker was still lurking. He doubted it—law enforcement was still on-site. But Holly's assailants had been relentless. They'd taken unnecessary chances.

To Seth, it seemed that whoever was after her was desperate. He knew from experience that desperate people could sometimes be unpredictable and reckless. And that rattled him to his core.

SIX

Walking into Seth's house, lugging Briar's cat carrier, felt oddly like coming home. It wasn't that the house was all that familiar to her, not yet. It was just so *welcoming*. The scent of lasagna and homemade bread clung to the air. The giggles of two happy children echoed from the family room. His mother greeted her with a tight hug, as did his sister-in-law, Cassie, whom Holly only vaguely knew from a decade ago.

She tried to push the welcoming feeling away. This was not her home. This would never be her home. In fact, if Eric's accusation came true, this would not even be Seth's home in the very near future.

Though they treated her like family, it would be wise of her to remember they weren't.

There was no reason for that thought to make her feel gloomy, yet it did. She pushed the feeling away. She had so much to be grateful for and needed to work harder at remembering that.

"You've had quite the time of it!" Julia exclaimed, misinterpreting her sadness for being troubled about her latest ordeal. "I've been thanking God over and over that He kept you safe today."

"Being shot at is the worst," Cassie lamented in a tone that implied she spoke from experience.

Before Holly could ask about that, Briar let out an aggrieved *meowwww* that caught Chloe's attention. She came running, far more interested in the surprise arrival of the cat than she was in her own mother.

Holly had to smile at that.

A young boy trotted behind her. His dark hair matched those of his father and uncle.

"This must be Wyatt," Holly said as the door opened behind her.

Seth strode in carrying the cat's plethora of supplies. A large bag of food, litter, the empty litter box. Traveling with a cat was no easy matter.

"It's my nephew all right," Seth said. "The most amazing little nephew on the planet."

Wyatt beamed at his uncle.

"He's my new friend," Chloe announced proudly. "We've been playing all day. You should see the ranch Wyatt's grandpa helped us build."

"It's awesome!" Wyatt said.

"I'm sure it is." Holly smiled at her daughter's new buddy. "I'll look at it pretty soon."

"I'm going to go set this stuff up in the laundry room. Let Briar get settled and I'll be right back."

Seth trudged off as Chloe scampered up to the carrier.

"Hi, Briar. I missed you." Her tone was full of delight. She glanced up at Holly. "Can she come out?"

"Of course."

Chloe opened the door, and the cat sauntered through the opening as if she already owned this new abode. Wyatt knelt next to Chloe, and the two of them showered Briar with adoration.

"We have four cats." Wyatt beamed proudly. "A

momma had three babies in our barn last spring. We were supposed to give one to Uncle Seth, but the kitty didn't want to leave his sisters, so Seth let us keep him."

"Can I see them someday?"

Wyatt shrugged. "Sure, Chloe. They're big now. Not as big as your cat, though."

It eased Holly's worry a bit to see that Chloe seemed unfazed by yesterday's attack. She was grateful for Wyatt's visit and the normalcy it brought to her daughter's day.

Cassie caught Holly's eye and motioned toward the kitchen. Julia and Holly followed her.

"I'm so sorry you've had such a rough time of it. Do the police have any leads?"

Holly remembered that Cassie was a private investigator, though at the moment, she was a very pregnant private investigator. Seth had mentioned Cassie and Eric were expecting twins in a few months. No wonder the woman had a blissfully happy glow about her.

Holly didn't want Cassie to get herself involved in anything dangerous, so she was hesitant to share too much information. The woman's intent, intelligent gaze made Holly think she'd like to dive into the case.

"They don't have much to go on," Holly admitted.

"It might be a while before they catch whoever is after you, so you should take this."

Cassie pulled what looked like a hot pink vial out of her pocket.

"What is that?" Seth asked as he strode into the kitchen.

"Bear spray." Cassie pressed it into Holly's palm. "It's a great deterrent."

Holly's fingers curled around the vial. She knew Cassie's intent wasn't for her to use it on an actual bear.

Seth frowned. "Those men aren't going to get close enough to her for her to use it."

Cassie smiled reassuringly. "Of course not."

"Just in case." Julia patted her shoulder comfortingly. "It's better to be prepared."

Holly knew Julia was right. "Thank you."

The front door opened, closed. They stopped talking and turned toward the kitchen doorway expectantly. Before Holly had the chance to be concerned, a tall strawberry blonde strode into the kitchen.

It had been years since Holly had last seen Nina, the youngest Montgomery sibling. The spunky teenager she recalled was now a gorgeous woman. While the boys had inherited James's dark good looks, Nina favored her mother's coloring.

"I never thought I'd have to show my ID to get on the property." She sounded more flustered than annoyed. "I even know Officer Rollins. He had to look over my driver's license anyway."

"He's just doing his job," Julia said.

"Why are you here?" Seth narrowed his eyes at Nina. "I thought I said it was safer for you if you stayed away."

Nina lifted a black leather bag. Holly knew she was a registered nurse and had a hunch the bag held medical supplies.

"I'm here because of you." Nina arched a brow at him. "I know you got stitched up recently. Last night, correct? You're at risk of popping your sutures if you don't take it easy. Mom said you got in a tussle today, too."

"Not a tussle," Seth corrected.

No, Holly thought, but she had been flung into him. She grimaced as she recalled his grunt of pain. Then he'd pursued a man through the woods.

"Are you here to check him out?"

"I sure am." Nina smiled at Holly. "By the way, it's good to see you again."

"Likewise." Holly appreciated the greeting even though she couldn't imagine Nina was too excited about her big brother getting hurt on Holly's behalf.

Nina crooked her finger at Seth. "Come on now. Let's go look at that wound."

Seth opened his mouth, clearly ready to protest, so Holly gave him a little nudge.

"For me? I feel terrible you got hurt on my account. I'd appreciate having a professional look you over."

Nina nodded approvingly.

The entire group of women looked at Seth expectantly.

He groaned, knowing he was outnumbered, then left the room with Nina.

"Where did my other son run off to?" Julia glanced around as if she just now realized Eric hadn't joined them. "I thought he was with you and Seth."

"He had an errand to run," Holly replied.

"He's getting Holly a phone." Cassie pulled open the oven door to peek at the lasagna, then closed it again. "He shouldn't be long. We can eat as soon as he's here."

"A phone? For me?" She was startled by Eric's thoughtfulness. In fact, Seth's whole family had been nothing but thoughtful. Holly's gratitude nearly overwhelmed her. They were sheltering her, Chloe, even their cat. Julia and James hadn't hesitated to offer to watch Chloe when Holly needed to leave. Seth had said she could use his laptop, since hers was destroyed. Cassie had given her bear spray, and now Eric was getting her a phone. She couldn't remember the last time anyone had taken care of her.

Typically, taking care of others was *her* job.

"It's only a pay-as-you-go phone." Cassie sounded

apologetic. "But we both felt you shouldn't be without a phone right now. That seemed to be the simplest option."

Holly would text Skylar, the foster child she was assigned to, her new number as soon as she got the phone set up.

"That's so kind of you to think of me. It's hard to be without a phone these days. We rely on them for everything."

"Isn't that the truth," Cassie said.

Holly had a sudden longing to be part of this big, caring family.

She had Chloe and Aunt Viv, who was nearing ninety and resided in an assisted living facility. It suddenly didn't feel like nearly enough.

Cassie glanced out the window. "Eric's here."

Holly was grateful to be put to work setting the table, though the mundane task was not enough to get her mind off longing for more. Not that it mattered. Seth was leaving.

Not just leaving the ranch, but leaving Mulberry Creek. He'd made it clear to his brother that it was important to him and no one had the right to try to stop him. Least of all, Holly. Not that she would ever consider asking. She'd thrown his life for a loop years ago, and she would never do that to him again.

Now was not the time to let herself get caught up in what-ifs and could-have-beens.

He'd loved her once, years ago. As he'd said…a lifetime ago. She'd hurt him by walking away. She didn't deserve him, or his kindness, now. Most important was the fact that while her pesky feelings toward him seemed to be growing, rekindling, he had given no indication that the same was true for him.

She would settle for his protection, his friendship, and she would be grateful for it.

Seth hoped his rambunctious family hadn't been too much for Holly. Her gaze had darted around the dinner table as she'd tried to keep up with the never-ending conversation. He had to assume it was quite a change from meals with only Chloe.

Now the house was quieter.

Eric had taken his family home.

After *tsking* over Seth's wound, applying butterfly bandages for added support and then joining them for dinner, Nina had left as well. Though Seth hadn't been happy she'd come to the ranch, because he worried about her safety, he did appreciate her support. It was also a relief to have his wound bandaged more securely. Though he would never admit it to anyone, it had hurt something fierce when Holly had collided with him.

James and Julia had retreated to their bedroom. They were likely decompressing from the busy day while reading before bed, as Seth knew was their nightly routine.

Chloe had dozed off. Holly had carried her into his office where she was now tucking her into bed for the night.

Two officers were outside patrolling. It was probably more than the department should spare right now, yet it was becoming obvious the attackers had no intention of stopping their pursuit of Holly.

Detective Bianchi had insisted on the extra overnight protection. Seth wasn't sure how long the department would be able to keep it up. For tonight, he was grateful.

The fire crackled in the hearth, casting a butterscotch glow across the room. It seemed strange that it could be so peaceful here while everything else felt so chaotic.

Seth glanced up as Holly shuffled back in.

"Did you get Chloe settled?"

"I did. I'm envious of the fact that she sleeps like a rock." Holly settled onto the sofa across from him. "Thank you for letting us bring Briar."

He glanced down at the fluffy, heavy cat that was snoozing in his lap. "No problem."

"Would you believe Briar was just an itty-bitty thing when I found her?"

He smiled, trying to picture it. The cat was bigger than some small dogs. "Really?"

"It's true." She nestled back in the cushions, looking weary. "I woke up one morning to the most pitiful sound. It took me a while to figure out where it was coming from. Finally, I opened the front door and there, curled up in a tiny, half-frozen ball, was this little pile of fluff. I scooped her up, held her to my chest while I rubbed her with my hand to try to warm her. I rushed her to the vet, who wasn't very optimistic because she was hypothermic. Needless to say, after many sleepless nights that included midnight feedings and endless cuddles, I realized she was going to make it."

Holly glanced adoringly at the cat she had rescued.

Seth was even more grateful he'd had the foresight to bring Briar to the ranch. It was clear the animal meant a lot to Holly.

"How long have you been back in Mulberry Creek?" Holly detoured the conversation in a direction he hadn't expected it to go.

"A little over a year."

"And you're ready to take off again so soon?"

Unlike Eric, there was no censure in Holly's tone.

He shrugged. "There's not much keeping me here."

With two fingers she flicked at the fringe of the throw pillow next to her. She gazed at it instead of returning her attention to him. "I take it that means there's no one special in your life."

"Not at the moment."

Was she just making conversation? Catching up with an old friend? Or was she asking because she was...interested? He doubted it. She'd made it clear years ago that they were too different. Not a good fit. Not the sort of couple who could last. Her cool demeanor made it hard to tell why she was asking. His heart seemed to kick in his chest, and he knew he shouldn't care why she was asking.

She'd shattered his heart once before.

Left him, left town, without any warning at all.

Now he was the one who had plans to leave. Tucker was counting on his partnership. The details were almost finalized. Seth had a plan, and it did not include Holly. It didn't include an adorable, energetic little girl. It didn't include an enormous, lovable cat.

He didn't need this complication.

Still, he would never kick Holly or her daughter out in their time of need.

He was going to have to work a little harder at corralling his feelings and guarding his heart.

She glanced at him then, blatant curiosity etched across her features. "Have you ever gotten serious with a woman?"

"A few times. Eventually the relationships fizzled out." He didn't think he needed to give more of an explanation than that. He knew he shouldn't be wondering the same about her. Apparently he couldn't help himself. "And you?"

He almost wished he hadn't asked. He should be working on keeping his distance. This sort of conversation was the opposite of keeping his distance. It was getting to know each other again on a personal level.

"I thought Connor might be the one." Her expression was bland when she spoke, as if she was completely over the relationship. "We dated for over two years then finally had to admit we wanted very different things out of life."

"How so?" He told himself he didn't really want to know, that he was just trying to be polite by keeping the conversation going. But truth be told, he found himself craving information about Holly. He wanted to know more.

He wanted to know everything.

This was not good. Not good at all.

He couldn't help himself.

"I wanted kids." She paused. "He did not."

"That's a pretty big thing to disagree on." Even back at the tender age of seventeen, Seth and Holly had talked about getting married, having children. He had known she wanted a big family. Lots of people to love. Probably because she'd had so little love herself while she'd had so very much love to give.

Of course a man not wanting children would be a deal breaker for her.

"It is a very big thing. Early on he told me how he felt. I was so baffled by that, literally could not even grasp the concept that he was serious. I naively thought he'd change his mind. Ironically, he thought I would change my mind. Before we knew it, a few years had gone by, and needless to say, we both stood firm in our convictions. We decided to go our separate ways."

"Are you still friends?"

She shrugged. "He was all about his work. He was a lawyer here in town, then got hired by a big firm in Denver and moved out of state. We parted on good terms though we haven't bothered to keep in touch."

"That had to be tough, ending things after that long."

"I don't know. I think a part of me realized it may not work out. I think I guarded my heart, knowing we had such a big difference between us."

"And now you don't date."

Her brow furrowed.

"That's what you told Mateo."

"I haven't, no. Not since Chloe came into my life. She had been in and out of foster care for years, and was dealing with a lot of trauma. Bonding with her and getting her the services she needed to heal has been a top priority. It's been very time-consuming. Worth it, yet time-consuming."

"She's doing well now?" Seth didn't know a whole lot about kids, but Chloe seemed well-adjusted to him. He could only assume that the child had flourished under Holly's nurturing.

"She's doing great and has been for a while now." She tugged a hand through her hair. "In fact, she's doing so well I was able to resume being a CASA after stepping away for a while."

He wished she didn't look so pretty. So absolutely beautiful in the flickering glow of the flames dancing in the hearth.

I don't need the complication, he reminded himself. *I finally have my life planned out.*

She doesn't date.

Chloe is her priority.

She's not interested in you.

He needed to pound these sentiments into his head. It didn't matter that she still made his heart race. *They* were never going to happen.

Still, he had a hundred more questions he wanted to ask her. How had Chloe come into her life? Why had she decided to become a CASA? How had she become a forensic accountant? What had finally brought her to Jesus, when Seth's own faith years ago had not been enough to sway her?

And the biggest question of all…

Why had she been so heartless when she left him?

He mentally bit his tongue, unwilling to ask her any of these things. He was too afraid it would bridge the gaping chasm between them. It was too late for that. There was no sense in getting to know Holly all over again.

You are leaving, he scolded himself. Then repeated it a few more times, lest his traitorous heart forget that very pertinent fact.

Holly shifted in her seat and leaned toward him.

"I want to tell you how sorry I am for the way I ended things."

He shrugged, pretending that the abruptness of it didn't still sting all these years later. "You were right. We were young. Too young to be serious. We never would have lasted."

She bit her lip, as if she wasn't sure what to say. She looked distraught, and despite himself, he wanted to comfort her.

"Although I will admit it was a blow that you just wrote me a letter and disappeared." He immediately wished he could take the accusatory words back, because there was no point in getting into this now, all these years later. She hadn't even delivered the letter herself. It had come in the mail. Yeah, it had been a low blow all right.

"I was a coward." Her gaze drifted over his face, then she glanced toward the fire. "I couldn't face you."

"I went to your house. I begged your dad to tell me where you'd gone." Seth ignored the hollowness building in his chest as he remembered that day. "He laughed at me. Then slammed the door in my face."

Holly winced. "He didn't know where I was. I needed a clean break."

"So your letter said." He hated how bitter he sounded, even after all this time. "Looks like you got it. Your life turned out well. Your clean break paid off."

She reached a hand out as if to take his, then seemed to think better of it and pulled it back.

"Seth, I am so sorry about the way I handled things. All I can say is that I was young. There was a lot about my life you didn't know back then. When I said I needed to get away, it wasn't from you."

"Really?" He struggled to keep his tone flat. "That's not how the letter read."

She opened her mouth to speak, then the low ring of Seth's phone caused her to clamp her jaw shut again.

He shifted the snoozing cat, winced at the persistent ache in his side from the knife wound and reached for the phone he'd left on the coffee table.

He hoped it wasn't Tucker. His friend had called this morning before they'd left for the park. Seth had sent off a quick text letting him know he was in the middle of something and would get in touch with him as soon as possible. He hated putting him off, but he had too much going on right now to give Tucker—the business—the required attention.

He glanced at the screen.

This, however, wasn't Tucker.

"It's Detective Bianchi."

"I need to text him my new number," Holly muttered. "Maybe there's been a break in the case."

"Hi, Mateo. I've got Holly with me. You're on speakerphone again."

"I have bad news." He hesitated a beat, and Seth could

picture him wincing. "Barry Ellis, the man who ran Holly off the road and tried to kidnap Chloe, has escaped."

Holly gasped, her eyes widening as she leaned forward, staring at the phone. "What? How? How is that possible?"

"Escaped?" Seth repeated. "From his cell?"

"We have surveillance cameras. They seem to have malfunctioned over the time period of his disappearance."

"Really?" Seth was skeptical. "Malfunctioned?"

"I suspect they were tampered with."

"By who? Who would have access?"

The detective didn't answer Seth.

"Someone from within your department?"

"I didn't say that."

"You're not denying it," Seth volleyed back.

"I'm not saying much of anything," Mateo corrected. "It's an active investigation. I give you my word I'm looking into it. I wanted to let you know what happened. I'll be in touch."

He disconnected.

Seth's eyes locked with Holly's. The terror he saw there ripped at his heart.

"Someone got to him inside of a cell. No wonder he wasn't talking. He probably knew if he held out long enough, someone would get him out." Her eyes widened. "Does that mean there's a dirty cop?"

"Possibly." Seth hated the idea yet knew it was likely. He didn't want to speculate too much. He had the utmost respect for law enforcement. But he knew that while the majority of people—cops included—were good at heart, there were always some who weren't. "I don't know who all could have access. A receptionist? A guard? A custodian?"

Holly pulled in a breath. "Now he's free to come after me again."

"Maybe he'll smarten up and realize the best thing for him to do is hightail it out of town."

"Although it really doesn't matter. He was locked up and someone still shot at me and broke into my home to steal my laptop. I don't think it's enough for the henchmen to get caught. This won't end until we figure out who the mastermind is behind it all."

He agreed with her, yet he didn't want to say that out loud, as if acknowledging it would somehow grant these men more power over her.

Seth wanted to tell her it would be okay. He couldn't because he refused to lie to her, refused to make promises he couldn't keep. Suddenly the conversation they'd had about the past seemed as if it didn't even matter. What mattered was here, now, the fact that someone had the resources to break a man out of jail.

Glancing toward the heavily curtained picture window, he no longer thought the two patrolling officers were enough. He knew it was going to be another sleepless night.

SEVEN

Seth had slept fitfully, managing a few short naps in between walking the perimeter of his yard after notifying the officers each time he'd be doing so. He desperately needed caffeine. He stopped short in the doorway when he realized Holly was sitting at the kitchen table. The sight of her took him back. Hair pulled into a tight ponytail on top of her head. A chewed-on pencil—a bad habit that she apparently still hadn't broken—clenched between her teeth. Paperwork of some sort in front of her.

She glanced up at him as her brow furrowed. "What?"

He shook his head and blew out a breath. "Nothing. I need some coffee."

"I don't think you've ever lied to me before." She tapped the pencil against the notepad.

"I haven't." He frowned.

"Then don't start now." Her analytical gaze skimmed over him. "Tell me what put that look on your face when you walked through the kitchen door."

He poured his coffee, coffee that Holly apparently had brewed, then dropped into the chair across from her.

"For a moment when I walked in, it felt as if I was walking straight into the past. Different kitchen. Different table. But your hair in a ponytail like you used to wear."

He nodded toward the pencil and smiled. "A chewed-up pencil. A pile of papers. It reminded me of the old days."

She glanced at the pencil and wrinkled her nose. "Nasty habit that helps me think." Then she looked back up at him. "A lot of things have brought the past roaring back the last few days. For me, at least."

"Me, too." Not his feelings, though, he told himself. He was holding those old feelings at bay. As he'd been tossing and turning last night, he'd been unable to stop their conversation from replaying in his mind. Holly's apology, nearly a decade in coming, had felt like a salve to the scars on his heart. It hadn't been just her words, but the sincerity of her expression, the look of sadness in her eyes.

What had she meant when she'd said there were things in her life that he hadn't known about?

He wanted to ask, and another part of him wanted to let it go, to leave the past in the past.

They could move forward. As friends.

Just friends.

*Liar…*a voice whispered through his mind. Fine. He realized it was a lie, but he was only lying to himself. He'd have to work harder at warding off those old feelings and not allowing them to resurrect. They needed to stay dead. Buried.

"Your family." She sighed. "They're so great. So warm. So welcoming. So…loving. I've missed them."

What about me? Did you miss me, too?

He could hardly ask that. Instead, he decided to keep the topic on safe ground. Besides, he was better off not knowing.

"I'm not surprised you became an accountant. Numbers were always your thing. I couldn't have asked for a better math tutor."

She laughed. "You thought you could flirt your way through our sessions."

"You were immune to my charms."

"That baffled you more than the Pythagorean theorem," Holly teased.

It was true.

"I thought I had to try harder to win you over. The harder I tried, the more you resisted."

Holly blushed. "I couldn't believe you were really interested in me."

He shrugged. "I wasn't, initially. I was hoping to bluff my way through the tutoring sessions. Then you became far more intriguing than the formulas you were trying so hard to teach me."

That was definitely true.

He had quickly realized Holly was smart, funny, beautiful. The whole package. He'd become determined to win her over.

She'd been just as determined to not let him.

"What changed? You never did tell me. I asked you out every tutoring session for two months before you finally agreed."

A soft smile flittered across her face.

"At first, I thought you were messing with me. I mean, you were *Seth Montgomery*." She emphasized the words, fluttering her lashes playfully. "All the girls wanted to date you. The boys wanted to befriend you. I couldn't imagine what you wanted to do with me. I was afraid you were trying to prank me." She turned serious. "Then one day, I was at the library, trying to open the stubborn old combination on my bike lock. I saw an elderly lady down the street. She was holding grocery bags, trying to cross. No one was stopping. Then all of a sudden, this truck pulls over. You hop out. Not only did you stop traffic, but you took her arm and helped her across the street."

He blinked at her. He'd done that? He didn't remember.

"You didn't do it for praise or attention. I knew then that you did it because you were a nice guy." She shrugged. "You won me over that day without even knowing it. The next time you asked me out, I said yes."

If I was so great, why did you ditch me? The words were dangling on the tip of his tongue, begging to be said.

His phone, which he'd placed on the table, announced an incoming call.

Tucker's name lit up the screen. It seemed to glare up at him, accusing. His friend had given him a day, but Seth had to assume there was a pressing matter. Probably paperwork of some sort that needed to be straightened out.

"You should get that." Holly clearly recognized the name. All the nostalgia had melted from her tone. She was all business again. "You don't want to put off your future business partner. He could be calling about something important."

"I'll call him later." He wished they could return to the conversation they'd been having. They wouldn't. The moment for reconnecting was over.

If it had ever been there at all.

It's for the best. You're leaving. She's not interested in you.

The mental pep talk jerked him back to reality.

"What are you working on?"

"I'm trying to recreate the conversation I had with the mystery lady." She motioned toward the notebook, which Seth could see was covered with her small, precise handwriting. "I was hoping that if I wrote the conversation down, it would shake something loose in my memory. I was hoping I'd remember a clue that would help me figure out who the lady is. Or who recommended me. Or what she was really calling about."

"It's not going well?"

She shook her head, frustrated. "I didn't come up with anything new. The woman was discreet. Too discreet. Nothing stands out as a clue."

Seth could feel her frustration. It troubled him that they had so little to go on. He had faith in the local police department, yet he knew it was going to be nearly impossible to solve this case with the limited information that they had.

Holly frowned. "Knowing that Barry Ellis escaped, I feel like this case is moving backward instead of forward."

Seth didn't want to say it out loud, but he couldn't agree more.

It was hard not to be disheartened this morning. Holly had felt off-kilter since finding out that Barry Ellis had escaped. Or maybe she felt off-kilter because Seth seemed intent on bringing up the past. She knew her apology was long overdue, and she should have done a better job of it last night. At least it was a start at righting her wrongs of the past.

Fortunately, Seth was not the sort of person to hold a grudge.

He'd even made Chloe a quick breakfast of toast and a sliced banana before his parents had bundled her up to take her to the other side of the ranch. She was anxious to visit her new friend, Wyatt, and the four barn cats he was so proud of.

Seth had offered to make Holly breakfast as well, even though food was the last thing on her mind.

"Don't stress yourself out over Barry Ellis." Seth knew

it was easier said than done. "It seems bleak right now, but Mateo's bound to get a break in the case sooner rather than later."

"Do you think so?"

"I do." Seth gave a nod of assurance. "I know it's easy to feel a little stir-crazy when we're stuck in the house like this. Maybe we could go over to Eric's to check out the cats with Chloe."

"I hate this feeling," Holly admitted. "I want to be doing something. I want to help Mateo somehow."

"I get that. The best way to help Mateo right now is to stay safe."

There was truth in Seth's words, so Holly didn't argue.

She was gathering up her papers when her phone rang. So far, other than Seth and his family, she'd given her new number to Skylar, Detective Bianchi and Georgina, her supervisor.

"Who is it?" He clearly expected it to be important since he was aware that she had given limited people her new number.

Holly glanced at her phone and though the number wasn't programmed in, she recognized it.

"It's Lori, our administrative assistant. She must have a question about one of the files I'm working on. I need to get this."

She answered, expecting Lori to have a work-related question. Georgina had approved Holly's request for a few days off. That meant her coworkers would need to step in on some of her current, most-pressing cases.

"Hi, Holly, I was going through the mail, and I came across something a little strange," Lori said. "Georgina gave me your new number. She said you would want me to call."

"Really? What is it?"

"Well, there was an envelope addressed to the office. Nothing unusual about that, so I opened it." She paused for effect. "Inside, there was an envelope addressed to you."

That got Holly's attention.

"Did you open the envelope addressed to me?"

"Should I?" Lori asked eagerly.

"No," Holly ordered. "In fact, don't touch the envelope any more than you already have."

Lori sighed, as if disappointed. "All right."

"Is there a return address?"

"No. It does show that it was mailed from Mulberry Creek yesterday."

Holly covered the receiver and updated Seth.

He hitched a brow.

Holly knew he was thinking what she was thinking. This could be the mysterious file from the unknown caller.

"What would you like me to do with it?" Lori asked. "Are you sure you don't want me to open it? I could scan the contents to you."

"If you don't mind, please put it on my desk." Holly figured if it was on her desk, out of Lori's sight, the woman wouldn't be as tempted to open it.

"I can do that."

"I'll be there shortly to see what's inside."

They disconnected, and she pocketed her phone.

"What's going on?"

"I think that Lori may have discovered the missing file. And I, for one, am anxious to see what's inside."

Seth felt confident that they had left the ranch without being followed. As far as he could tell, no one had figured out Holly was staying with him. Given the persistence of the criminals, he thought for sure the ranch would have been under attack by now if they knew she was there. He didn't know how long the reprieve would last, so he'd gladly take it.

An officer was periodically driving by the ranch during the day. Eric and James were keeping watch as well. Holly had a hard time leaving Chloe. She had to because she knew the mysterious envelope could be of great importance.

Seth noticed Holly checking her phone again.

"Nothing from the detective yet?"

She shook her head. "I know he's a busy man. I'm sure he'll see my text as soon as he has a free minute."

He glanced in his rearview mirror. A truck had turned onto the road behind them a few miles back. So far, it had kept a respectable distance. He didn't get the feeling that it was a threat. Still, he valued the importance of being vigilant. Danger could come when you least expected it. In a situation like this, it was best to never let your guard down.

The traffic grew heavier once they neared town. Still satisfied that they weren't being followed, Seth pulled up to the small, nondescript brick building that Holly had directed him to.

Her phone buzzed.

"It's Mateo." She read the text. "He's on his way."

"Should we go in? Or wait for him?"

"I'd rather go in. I don't think anyone knows we're here." Holly glanced around the nearly empty parking lot. A worry line rested between her brows. "I still feel so exposed."

So did he.

They stepped out into the cool autumn day. The sky was blue. The sun was shining. It was the perfect day for a stroll through the park, a picnic, a horse ride around the ranch. It didn't seem to be the sort of day for trying to track down a would-be murderer.

Seth followed Holly into the building. She was greeted by Lori, who seemed to have endless questions. Holly answered a few then politely excused herself so she and Seth could go to her office. The door was ajar. Holly didn't seem concerned by this.

Seth thought Lori was probably the last person inside the room.

Beige carpeting covered the floor, nearly matching the beige shade of the walls. A table and chairs took up one corner. Seth assumed that was where she met with clients.

Large, framed photos of vibrant landscapes decorated each wall, saving the space from being utterly dull.

Her desk was tucked off to the side.

It was no surprise that the top of the desk was immaculate. Holly seemed the type of person to tidy up every evening before leaving work. From here, he could see a desktop computer with an extra monitor, the back of a picture frame that he assumed held a picture of Chloe, and a large manila envelope.

Holly quickly crossed the room to take a look. He was only a step behind.

Just as Lori had said, the outer envelope was addressed to the accounting agency, with the agency's address listed. They could see a second envelope poking out from the first. Neither dared to touch it, though Seth knew they were both itching to do so.

"I can't wait to see what's inside," Holly said.

"I hope it's enough to figure out who's behind this."

Could this be it? Finally an answer to their prayers?

They heard murmuring out in the hallway.

Holly squinted at the door. "That sounds like Mateo."

A moment later, Lori led the detective into Holly's office.

He nodded a greeting. "Let's hope this is the break we've been waiting for."

Detective Bianchi placed his briefcase on the corner table, opened it and pulled out a pair of gloves and two evidence bags. Next, he pulled the inner envelope, the one addressed to Holly, free from the larger envelope. He placed the large envelope in an evidence bag.

"Are you ready to see what's inside?"

"More than ready." She opened her desk, took out a letter opener and handed it to Mateo. He carefully sliced open the top of the envelope then gently slid out the sheet of paper that it held. He placed it on Holly's desk.

Seth had been hoping for a clear-cut clue. Or better yet, a well-written explanation as to who was after Holly and why. This was not it. At least not for him. He glanced hopefully at Holly. She was frowning. His already dwindling hope fizzled and died.

"This isn't a scanned copy." Mateo traced a finger in the air, over the page, careful not to touch it. "You can see that the sheet is a bit crooked in the frame. And here—" he pointed to the left side "—looks like a slice of a table-top got into the frame. My assumption is that whoever sent this took a picture of the page then printed it off."

"This is it?" Holly looked crestfallen. "There's not another page? Nothing else in the envelope?"

Mateo double-checked, though they all knew he'd been thorough from the start.

"I'm afraid not."

"This isn't much to go on." Holly shook her head and sighed. "I'd hardly call this a file. As far as evidence goes, this is utterly disappointing. Did she really think this would be helpful?"

"We were all hoping for something a little more," Mateo seemed to search for the word, "substantial."

"This is so discouraging," Holly muttered.

"Do these numbers make any sense to you?" They meant absolutely nothing to Seth. Five columns of numbers that he couldn't make heads or tails of.

"It's a ledger of some sort, obviously. Without having a point of reference, since there's not even a title at the top of the columns, I'm not sure what I'm looking at." Holly glanced at Mateo. "You're right. This page looks as if someone took a picture of it. I think whoever did so accidentally cut off the top of the ledger. Which, in this case, could be the most important part. I don't know what these columns represent, and it's impossible to guess. They don't look like dates. There is nothing to hint which column represents dollar amounts, though most likely some must be. That's typically the point of a ledger."

Mateo arched a brow. "Think you can figure it out?"

Holly bit her lip, looking unsure, then she nodded. "I'm definitely willing to give it a try. Any chance I can get a copy of this?"

"I consider this evidence," Mateo said. "I want it handled as little as possible. I'd rather not run it through a copy machine until it's been dusted for prints."

Holly frowned and disappointment seemed to emanate from her.

"In the meantime—" the detective held up his cell phone "—let's see if I can get a clear shot to send you. I'll try to do a better job than whoever took the original photo."

Within minutes, Mateo had taken the photo, sent it to Holly's email and Holly was able to print the page on the workroom copier.

"What happens next?" Seth turned to Mateo.

"I'm bringing the envelopes in to have them processed. I'm hoping if we dust for prints, we'll get something off the inner envelope. I don't have high hopes for the outer envelope. I think it was handled too much. The postmark says Mulberry Creek, mailed yesterday, which fits our time frame. I'll have someone look into seeing if the post office can give us any insight as to where in town it was mailed from."

"How long will that take? I don't mean to be pushy. But, well, Holly's life seems to be on the line here."

"I know, Seth. I promise to make it a priority. I'll let you know as soon as I hear anything from the lab."

Holly glanced down at the paper she clutched in her hand. Her brow was furrowed, as if she was willing the random rows of numbers to make sense.

Mateo gave her arm a gentle squeeze. "It's not uncommon for a case to take a while to break. Don't be discouraged."

She offered up a weak smile.

"We *will* crack this case. I give you my word."

Seth didn't doubt the detective. He was sure they would catch the mastermind. Eventually. With the limited clue they'd been given, would it be soon enough?

EIGHT

Holly knew they should go back to the ranch. However, since they were out and about, there was a stop she really wanted to make. School had let out for the day, and Skylar hadn't responded to any of her recent texts. At seventeen, she could be moody, sulky. Other times she'd call Holly and chat her ear off. The fact she hadn't responded probably meant she was in one of her slumps, and Holly was worried about her.

"I need to make a stop before we go back to the ranch," she announced as they slid into the Prius. She started up her vehicle and glanced at Seth.

"I hope you don't want to go back to your house."

"I want to check in on Skylar."

"That's not a good idea. But I don't think you really want my opinion."

"Not this time. Sorry." She wrinkled her nose apologetically. "Skylar has been through a lot. She gets really down sometimes. I think now is one of those times since she's not responding to my texts. I tried calling her last night as well. Nothing. I called Alice, her current foster mom, and she confirmed that Skylar hasn't been herself the past few weeks. I want to see if there's anything I can do for her. She has a court date coming up soon. I'd like to check if that's what's bothering her."

Chances were, Skylar wouldn't talk. Still, Holly thought it was important for the girl to know she was there for her. She suspected the upcoming court date was what had Skylar in a slump. The girl's mother had died several years ago. Her father was in and out of jail and had no interest in her, yet he had refused to give up his rights.

Skyler was petitioning the courts, requesting his rights be terminated. Though she was almost eighteen, she claimed it was the principal of the matter. She wanted to feel as if she had some control over her own life.

He had never been a parent to her, and she wanted him to know she didn't think of him as such.

After a quick call to Alice, they made the short trip to her house. It was a small, white home on the edge of town, nestled in the middle of a block of houses. Alice worked as a teller at a local bank. She was able to work hours that allowed her to be home when Skylar got done with school.

When Holly parked at the curb she turned to Seth. Skylar's situation was confidential, and though Holly trusted Seth, she needed to honor that commitment. "I hate to ask, but would you mind waiting in the car?"

He frowned as he glanced up and down the street. So far, their trip to town had been uneventful. It was clear he suspected that might change.

"How about if I wait near the car?" he compromised.

"Okay."

As Holly walked up to the house, Seth leaned against the Prius. He had his phone out. She wondered if he was really checking messages, or pretending to look busy. It was probably the latter. She suspected he was being vigilant without appearing so. Her heart swelled with gratitude again as that feeling of being cared for washed over her.

Don't get used to it, she reminded herself.

The front door opened before she reached it, as if Alice had warned Skylar she was coming. The teen skulked out onto the front porch. Holly hadn't anticipated standing out in the open. Yet it was obvious Skylar was not about to invite her inside.

The petite teen seemed wary. She had shadows under her eyes, and looked like she hadn't slept for days. Her long blond hair was mussed as if she'd forgotten to brush it. She wore no makeup, which was very unlike her.

Holly was suddenly glad she'd thought to stop to check in on her.

"I haven't heard from you in a while." Holly tried to keep her tone conversational. "I've missed you. How are you?"

"Fine." Skylar's tone was clipped. She narrowed her eyes at Seth, who was still leaning against the car, doing his best to look unobtrusive. Given his large stature, he wasn't doing the best job of it. "Who's he?"

"Just a friend. He's stretching his legs but wanted to give us some privacy."

Skylar said nothing. She began toying with her charm bracelet, a cherished keepsake from her deceased mother, and stared off into the distance. Holly had been Skylar's CASA for several months now and had worked hard at building a strong rapport with the girl. But today she felt as if they didn't know each other at all. The distance between them concerned her, mostly because she wasn't sure what had caused it.

"I'm sure it's stressful knowing that the hearing is coming up."

Skylar shrugged. "He's never been a dad to me. It's not like anything will be changing. Not really, even if the court decides in my favor. But I was never able to be adopted because of him. It's like he doesn't want me but doesn't want anyone else to have me. I don't want him to have that kind of control over me. It's not fair."

"You're right." Holly nodded sympathetically. "It's not fair."

"I don't want to talk about it."

Holly tried asking about school, her friends, her part-time job at the health-food store in town.

Skylar continued to give clipped responses, and she seemed to grow more agitated by the moment. Holly glanced around, feeling a bit wary herself. It almost felt as if they were being watched. She glanced at Seth, and he immediately looked up from his phone, confirming her suspicions he wasn't really paying attention to it at all. He gave her a questioning look. Then he glanced down the street again.

Surely he'd realize if something were actually wrong?

She turned back around saw Alice watching them through the blinds. Holly cried out, surprised.

Skylar whirled, catching her foster mom as well.

Alice stepped away from the window, but Skylar looked rattled.

Holly's protective instincts kicked in.

"Is everything okay between you and Alice?"

"Yes." Skylar's annoyance was accentuated by the delicate rattle of the charms on her bracelet as she tossed her hands into the air.

"Skylar?" Holly pressed. "Is something other than the hearing bothering you? You know if anything is wrong, you can tell me. I'm here to support you, no matter what it is."

Skylar glanced over her shoulder again, as if concerned Alice was still watching. Then she shook her head. "I'm fine. Everything is fine."

Everything was clearly not fine.

Holly had the distinct impression that this was about more than the hearing. Skylar had talked to her in the past. Why would she clam up about it now? What had happened to make her suddenly block Holly out like this?

The teen winced as if she wanted to speak but couldn't quite get the words out. Then her eyes widened in surprise. Holly corkscrewed her neck to look over her shoulder.

A black car drove by slowly. She didn't know much about cars, but it looked expensive. The windows were tinted. It was impossible to see who was behind the wheel.

Skylar's already pale complexion seemed to turn gray as she stared at the car.

"What's wrong?" Holly demanded.

The driver halted at the stop sign. It sat there waiting though there was no other traffic. Then they stepped on the gas, and the car sped away. Was the driver someone to be concerned about? Or had they been distracted by their phone or maybe by a baby in the back seat? It was possible there was an innocent reason for their bizarre driving.

"Nothing is wrong!" Skylar exclaimed, backing toward the house.

"Yes, something is," Holly said, concerned. "Do I need to talk to Alice? Should I call Shelley?"

The girl blanched when Holly mentioned her caseworker.

Or was it the mention of her foster mother that had her rattled?

Holly couldn't be sure.

Yes, there was definitely more going on with Skylar than the upcoming hearing. Holly was certain of it.

"Who was in the car, Skylar? Is someone threatening you?"

"Leave me alone, okay?"

No, it was not okay. If the circumstances were different, if a killer weren't after Holly, she'd convince Skylar to go somewhere private where they could talk. There was a small café that Skylar liked because of their vegetarian menu and selection of green smoothies. If only Holly could get her alone, she might open up. But now was not the time for Holly to be bopping all over town.

If she was going to get Skylar to talk, now was her only chance.

"Is everything okay with Jordyn?" Jordyn was Skylar's younger half sister. Holly knew how much Skylar hated that they'd been separated. But Jordyn, who was four years younger and whose father had already given up rights, had gone to a family who hoped to adopt her.

They did not want Skylar, the older, supposedly troubled teen who had the added complication of a different biological father who had *not* given up his parental rights but who refused to step up and be the father he should be.

"What do you mean? Why are you asking about Jordyn?" Fear instantly laced Skylar's tone. "Is something wrong? Did you hear something?" She looked nearly frantic, her worry for her sister clear.

Holly reached out, gently rubbing Skylar's arm. "I haven't heard anything. I thought maybe her adoption was finalized. I thought maybe that's why you're so upset."

"I'm not upset," Skylar growled.

Holly glanced at the house again. "I think I should speak with Alice."

"No!" Skylar snapped. Her light blue eyes widened. In fear? Anger? "I'm fine. I'll be good. I'm staying out of trouble. Just leave me alone!"

She whirled and ran into the house. The door slammed behind her.

Holly's heart wanted to break. She longed to go after Skylar, didn't want to leave her alone when she was so upset, but would that only make matters worse?

"What was that about?" Seth strode up the sidewalk.

"I don't know." She wondered if she should speak with Alice. She was afraid that would not go over well with Skylar, and she didn't want to lose her trust. Though she felt as if she already had, and she had no idea why. "She's upset. Something is clearly wrong. I thought she liked Alice and Shelley. When I mentioned speaking with them, she seemed almost scared." She paused. "Did you notice the car that drove by?"

What had set Skylar off?

Was it the mention of Alice or Shelley as she originally thought…or could it have been the car?

"The car that rolled at a snail's pace to the stop sign? Sat there then tore off? Yeah. I texted Mateo the license plate number because something seemed off. I was tempted to follow them, but I didn't want to leave you alone after what's been going on." Seth glanced at the house. "Is she in trouble?"

Holly blew out a breath. "I think she might be."

Now she had not only her own problem to deal with, but she was sure something serious was going on with the teen as well. How was Holly going to clear her head enough to try to decipher the ledger that waited for her in the car?

Holly had agreed to let Seth drive them home. Primarily so she could look over the ledger she had received.

Seth could tell she was disturbed by her visit with the teen. She'd studied the ledger but had no idea what the numbers stood for.

Once they arrived at the ranch, he suggested she take a break from it, hoping that taking some time to clear her head might help them in more ways than one.

Though he'd tried to give them privacy, and he hadn't been able to hear their conversation, it had been clear from his vantage point that Skylar was a ball of nervous energy. Seth felt for the teen. He knew Holly was worried, but her role as a CASA kept her from saying too much. It was important to be respectful of that and he would try to support her any way he could.

Chloe and his parents had returned from Eric's by the time Seth and Holly arrived home.

When he'd mentioned taking Chloe out to see the horses, Holly had agreed it would be a good distraction. Seth thought it would be beneficial for mother *and* daughter.

Seth whistled, and his beautiful chestnut stallion, Echo, turned his head, paused then took off at a trot toward the fence line where Seth waited with Holly and Chloe.

"He's going to be expecting a treat," Seth told Chloe. "That's how I trained him to come to a whistle." He held out a baby carrot. "Do you want to give it to him?"

Chloe glanced at Holly, silently asking for permission.

Holly smiled, and Seth could almost see some of her tension melting away.

"You can feed him. Listen to Seth so you don't get your fingers nibbled."

Chloe's eyes widened, and she turned to him. "Will he nibble my fingers?"

Echo reached them, and Chloe backed away, unsure.

"Hold your hand like this." He demonstrated.

Chloe held her hand flat, fingers together. "I can't have my fingers apart or he'll think they're carrots."

Seth chuckled. "Exactly. Keep them together, and you'll be fine."

She still looked a bit cautious.

It was understandable. To a small girl the horse had to look gargantuan.

"Want me to lift you up?" He didn't really expect her to take him up on the offer.

Echo whinnied petulantly as he leaned his head over the fence expectantly. Seth scrubbed his neck, giving him some love while silently encouraging his four-legged friend to be patient.

"Yes, please." Chloe stretched her arms up toward Seth. "He's hungry."

He scooped the child up.

"Hey, Echo, ready for a treat?" Seth asked.

The horse nickered, seemingly in exasperation.

"Echo?" Chloe giggled. "That's a silly name."

"Silly?" Seth pretended to be terribly affronted. "It's not silly. It's the coolest name ever. You know how he got that name?"

Chloe shook her head.

"Because when this big, beautiful horse goes racing through the field his hooves hit the ground so hard the sound echoes."

Chloe's eyes widened. "That is pretty cool."

"I told you so," he said, his tone light and teasing.

Chloe held out her palm, the carrot balanced on top of her flat hand. The enormous horse nuzzled her, greedily snatching the carrot from her. Chloe gasped, surprised by the feel of the horse's velvety muzzle against her skin. She jumped, turned into Seth. Her chocolate chip cookie breath fluttered across his neck. She tightened her arms around him as if totally trusting him to protect her.

And he would.

He knew he'd do anything to keep this little one safe.

His heart was suddenly so full of longing. Longing for a different life than the one he'd been living. He'd concentrated on ranching since leaving the military. Even with his family nearby, it had been a lonely life. Lonely because it was missing what he hadn't allowed himself to realize he wanted.

A wife.

A child.

Many children, really.

His own close-knit family.

All this time he thought his heart had been craving action, adventure, some sort of superficial fulfillment. Now he realized that wasn't what he'd been missing at all.

It was in that moment that he knew without a doubt he wanted Holly and Chloe. Wanted them to be his. He wanted to be theirs.

It was too bad for him that Holly didn't seem to want the same thing. At least not with him.

"Do we have more carrots?" Chloe wondered as she slowly peeled herself off Seth and turned her attention back to the horse. "He's starving."

Echo reached toward her, his large nose sniffing snoopily.

Chloe giggled in delight. Seth's heart seemed to swell in his chest at the precious sound. He wished he could hear Chloe laugh every day. What was he going to do when they wrapped up this case and walked out of his life?

If his life had a gaping hole before, it would be monumentally worse when they went back to their own lives.

"I don't think he's starving. I'm sure Seth keeps him well-fed. He's like you." Holly tapped Chloe on the nose, making the girl grin. "He likes his treats."

"I have a few more." Shifting Chloe in the crook of his arm, Seth reached into his pocket and pulled out a handful of baby carrots. He allowed Chloe to feed Echo the half dozen he'd grabbed. He tried to push away the melancholy feeling that had come over him. He needed to enjoy this beautiful moment God had given him.

With one arm wrapped around Seth's neck, Chloe leaned toward Echo, holding out her other carrot-filled hand.

"I think she likes you." Holly gave Seth a gentle nudge.

"She's a pretty special girl," Seth said quietly.

Now that the carrots were gone, Chloe was rubbing Echo's neck, the horse's second favorite thing.

"I think she's pretty special, too." Holly met his gaze. Gratitude seemed to flow from her. "It's nice to hear someone else say it."

He hoped she realized he meant it. Chloe was a sweet kid. In the few short days they'd spent together, he could feel himself getting attached. He wished he could take this moment in time and freeze it. Hold on to it somehow. Both Chloe and Holly looked so happy, content. It seemed as if, for this moment at least, Holly had forgotten someone was trying to kill her.

As anxious as he was for the killer to be caught, he was going to miss being with her like this.

He was going to miss her and Chloe both. Truth be told, he'd even miss the needy cat that insisted on sleeping on his lap anytime he dared sit down.

He hoped the move to Bozeman when he joined Tucker would be a huge distraction, because he was going to need it.

"Could I maybe ride him someday?"

Seth wanted to tell Chloe yes, he'd love to take her out on a trail ride. He'd love to take her momma, too, if she was interested in coming along on one of the half dozen horses the ranch owned.

Before he could say so, Holly interjected.

"I don't think so." She gave Chloe's arm a gentle pat. "It's too dangerous right now. And Seth is moving soon."

Chloe turned to him, her brow furrowing in a way that reminded him of Holly. "Why are you moving? You have horses and cows, and the pasture has so many pretty flowers. Don't you love it here?"

The question was asked with the innocence of a child, and yet her words made so much sense.

He glanced at Holly.

She gave him an apologetic shrug. "I don't want her to be disappointed."

"And," Chloe continued as her eyes widened in delight, "you have such pretty birds here! Look, it's so shiny."

Seth swung his gaze upward, immediately spotting what Chloe found so fascinating.

"That's no bird," he muttered, his heart suddenly jackhammering. "We've got a problem."

"What's wrong?"

Their moment of quiet bliss was shattered.

"Take her inside. Now." Seth quickly transferred Chloe into Holly's arms. There was no time to explain. He loved that Holly trusted him enough not to argue. She took her daughter and rushed toward the house.

Seth pulled his Mag from his holster.

Pointed it at the object in the sky.

He knew exactly what a drone looked like. It had been

his idea to implement them on the ranch. Lost cow? Send out a drone. Not sure where the herd was grazing? Send out a drone. Think the wolf howls echoing across the pastures sounded a little too close to the newborn calves? Send out a drone for that, too.

While Eric had agreed, he'd been hesitant. He'd let Seth take charge.

That was how Seth knew this drone was not one of theirs. Eric didn't know how to operate the things. Besides, they were all stored here, on Seth's property.

This one cruising above, its metal frame shimmering when it hit the sun just right, had no business doing so.

Seth took aim.

Fired.

A fireball lit up the sky.

The resounding *boom was* so loud he felt his teeth rattle.

Chloe screamed, and he realized they hadn't quite reached the house yet.

Thank God Chloe had spotted the drone when she had, because this was not an ordinary drone.

Seth had heard enough bombs go off to realize he'd just shot into one, safely detonating it in the air rather than allowing it to crash into his house, which was clearly the intent. Still, debris scattered, falling from the sky. Blazing bits landed on the green grass in the pasture. He was grateful that at the sound of the gunshot the horses had bolted, running off into the distance and out of the range of the fiery bits raining down.

He took off toward the barn, his gaze scouring the horizon even as he ran. When he was sure it had been a lone drone, he darted into the barn. He pulled his own drone off the shelf, activated it and sent it off in the direction the intruding drone had emerged from.

He watched the screen that was built into the remote control. The drone was high-tech, as far as drones for personal use went. They needed it to be, to search for missing cattle. As it flew through the sky, offering the aerial display Seth had become adept at viewing, he steered it toward the road. While they had a decent range, even the best drone could only travel a few miles. The operator couldn't be that far off.

There. In the distance was a sporty black car. If he could only get the drone close enough to read the license plate, that would be ideal. He startled when he saw someone walk around the vehicle.

He wasn't surprised by their presence. He was surprised by the fact that, if he wasn't mistaken by the tall, lithe figure, it was a woman.

In an instant he realized what she was doing. She took a shooter's stance. Raised a gun and…he heard the report of a gunshot in the distance.

The screen in his hand went black.

He let out an angry growl, knowing his own drone had been shot down and was now spiraling to the ground.

Spiraling, ready to crash and burn, just like his hope of getting more information. Even worse, now he knew for a fact that Holly's pursuers knew she was at the ranch. Did they also know that the ranch was under police guard? The car wasn't on the road that led to the driveway, but rather on the road that ran parallel, clear on the other side of the property.

Even more surprising was that he was sure the black car was the same black car that had rolled past Skylar's this afternoon.

But why?

Had the car followed him and Holly from her office? Had they not noticed they were being tailed?

Or was the teenager involved somehow?

Seth didn't see how that was possible, but right now, he wasn't certain about anything.

NINE

Knowing a homemade bomb had almost hit the ranch several days ago left Holly shaken. Sure, she, Chloe and Seth had been outside looking at the horses, but James and Julia had been in the house. And what if the blast radius had been enough to kill them all?

What a horrific thought.

Holly could not stop thanking God for their protection, for surely, He had been watching over them all.

A team had come out to collect the debris.

Mateo had expanded the patrol around the sprawling ranch, and while Holly felt guilty about the extra strain it put on the small force, she was grateful for it.

The weekend had passed by uneventfully. Probably because they'd hunkered down, taking refuge at Big Sky Ranch.

Now Mateo was here with more information to share.

Holly clenched her hands into fists and placed them on her lap so she wouldn't nervously tap her fingers on the kitchen table.

"I'm going to get right to it." Holly appreciated Mateo's directness. "There was a pipe bomb attached to the drone, as Seth suspected."

Seth nodded.

"There was a timer, so I'd say whoever set it estimated how long it would take to fly it to the house. Maybe it was to land on the roof or fly through a window," Mateo continued. "There's no telling what the exact plan was, but the intent is clear."

Yes, it sure was. The intent was to kill them all.

Holly shuddered.

"What about the car? Any leads on it?"

"Not yet, Seth, unfortunately. Not a lot of people use surveillance cameras around here. The town itself doesn't use CCTV, though I've pushed for it," Mateo admitted. "The interesting thing, and I say that with a fair amount of sarcasm, is that the license plate number you gave me belongs on an old Ford Pinto."

"That car was not a Pinto. They don't even make those anymore." Seth frowned. "I would've paid closer attention to the make and model if I hadn't been so sure the license plate would give us the information we needed."

"One of my men contacted the owner, went right to his house. The car belongs to a young guy, and he was surprised to see the plates had been swiped right off his car. He hadn't even noticed. Whoever tried to bomb this place was thinking ahead. They knew you'd see the license plate and didn't care because it wouldn't matter."

Seth scrubbed a hand through his hair.

Another dead end.

He looked as frustrated as Holly felt.

"I do actually have some good news," Mateo continued. "I received confirmation that we have a match on the prints lifted from the envelope."

"Who is it?" Holly leaned forward.

"They belong to a woman from Mulberry Creek. Teresa Krause. Sound familiar?"

Holly's brow furrowed in thought. "No."

"What do you know about her?" Seth asked Mateo.

"She's a fifty-eight-year-old widow. Her son, Todd, lives in Bozeman. We haven't been able to get in touch with him yet but we only found out an hour ago."

"Todd... Todd Krause?" Holly pieced together the information.

"Correct," Mateo confirmed. "Do you know him?"

"His name is familiar." Holly began flipping through her mental Rolodex. She knew that name. She was sure of it.

"Up until last year, he lived in Mulberry Creek. Just moved to Bozeman a few months ago."

"Yes." Holly slammed a hand against the table in excitement. "I remember now. He was a client of mine."

Being cognizant of client confidentiality, she didn't tell him that Todd had come to her concerned that his business partner was skimming money from their profits. He'd hired Holly. She'd found the evidence to corroborate his suspicion.

"He could have recommended you to his mother," Mateo said. "That could be our link, right there. Unfortunately, Teresa seems to be missing. We checked with her neighbors, and they haven't seen her the last few days. They suggested she could be visiting Todd. Apparently she does that often. It could be that's why we can't get a hold of him right now, either."

"I hope that's the case." Holly's tone held concern.

Her phone rang. She intended to ignore it but then realized that so few people had her new number, it must be important.

"You can take that, if you need to," Mateo said.

She glanced at the phone. She recognized the number. It was Shelley, Skylar's caseworker.

"I do need to take it." She apologetically excused herself to the hallway. "Shelley? Is everything okay?"

"Yes, now it is," Shelley said. "Judge Cromwell shifted his schedule around. He moved up Skylar's hearing. He wants to hold it this afternoon. He didn't let me know until late last Friday. I tried calling you over the weekend but wasn't able to get through. Then when I spoke with Alice this morning, she said you called her from a new number recently. Fortunately she was able to retrieve it from her phone. I know it's short notice, but can you make it today?"

"I'm sorry about the number, I should have thought to let you know. Life has been a bit hectic lately." She cut herself off there. Shelley wasn't calling to talk about Holly. This was about Skylar. "Yes, I'll make this afternoon work. Give me the details."

Five minutes later, she was seated at the table with Seth and Mateo again.

Mateo and Seth had clearly been discussing the drone and the explosion.

They turned their attention to her.

She cringed, knowing neither man was going to appreciate what she had to say.

"I need to be at the courthouse in three hours. Skylar's hearing got moved up. I cannot miss it."

Especially now, when Skylar was so obviously struggling with something. Even though the girl was pushing her away, she clearly needed Holly more than ever. Whether Skylar thought so or not.

"Is this a CASA situation?" Mateo asked.

"It is."

Seth said nothing, though Holly could tell he wasn't pleased about more time away from the ranch. It was a risk, but one she felt strongly she needed to take.

Mateo turned to Seth. "You'll go with her? Keep her safe?"

"You know I will."

While Holly wished she didn't need his protection, she was grateful for it.

As promised, Holly showed up at the courthouse that afternoon. She'd changed out of the jeans she'd been wearing at the ranch. The day had turned cold and dreary with sleet spilling from the sky. She now wore a cozy wool pantsuit that was more appropriate for the courthouse. And the weather.

She spotted Skylar sitting on a bench outside of the courtroom. She wore black leggings and a baggy sweater, which, for her, counted as dressing up. Shelley, her caseworker, and Alice, her foster mother, stood a good distance away. They were whispering frantically to each other.

"Seth, I'm going to let them know I'm here."

"I'll find somewhere to wait."

Holly strode toward the women. The moment they spotted her, they stopped talking and took a step away from one another. They looked almost…guilty. Holly frowned. The three of them should be working together as advocates for Skylar. Why did she suddenly feel like an outsider?

A quick glance at the scowling teen suggested that she, too, felt like an outsider.

"Can I speak with Skylar for a moment? Alone?" The question was directed to the two other women, but Holly didn't wait for an answer.

She motioned for Skylar to follow her, not really expecting her to, but the girl jumped to her feet. Holly led her to a side room that they had used on other occasions. They entered it, and Holly shut the door.

This time, she didn't start with questions.

She pulled Skylar into a gentle hug. "I've been worried about you."

To her surprise, Skylar leaned into her, almost melted really, into her comforting embrace. She was even more surprised when Skylar, who always came across so tough, let out a sniffle. Holly released her, reached into her purse and handed her a tissue. The teen took it and dabbed at her nose.

"Skylar, you need to talk to me," Holly said gently. "I can't help if I don't know what the problem is."

"I want to live with you," Skylar blurted. "Can I? I heard you and Shelley talking one time. I know you're licensed for foster care. Please? I won't be any trouble. I'll be good. I'll help around the house."

"I don't have an extra bedroom." It was simpler to say that than saying she didn't have a house right now. At least not one where she felt safe. She couldn't burden Skylar with her troubles, nor could she get into her living situation with the girl.

"I'll sleep on the sofa. You can stuff me in the closet!" Skylar nearly wailed.

"Skylar, I would never stuff you in the closet." To anyone else, it may have sounded like a silly suggestion. But Holly knew the girl's history. Holly knew she'd been locked in the closet as punishment…and worse.

"You don't want me."

"It's not that," Holly said gently. Oh, how could she possibly explain this? "There was an accident at my house." Not exactly an accident, yet there was no other way to discreetly describe a man with a broken nose bleeding all over her kitchen floor. "I'm not staying there right now. I have to stay with a friend until I get the situation ironed out."

Skylar stiffened, and Holly knew she had lost the girl.

"Are you unhappy living with Alice?" Holly knew there weren't many other options. There were too many foster children and too few homes, but if there was a legitimate issue, Holly would need to look into it.

Skylar didn't seem to hear her.

"Skylar?"

"Kiana didn't run away," Skylar said, speaking of the foster girl whom Holly had served as CASA before being paired with Skylar. The assignment had been brief, and she'd only met Kiana twice. Kiana and Skylar had known each other as they'd been in the same group home. Before Kiana had disappeared and Skylar had moved in with Alice.

Holly frowned. "There was a note."

"So what?"

"She's been gone for at least three months. If she didn't run away, where did she go?"

"Never mind." Skylar pulled away. "Forget I said anything." The girl pivoted and flew out the door.

Holly hurried after her.

Seth was waiting a respectable distance away, but in her rush, Skylar nearly collided with him. He held out his hands to steady her.

"You okay?"

She nodded, but tugged her arms from his grip. "Are you Holly's friend?"

"I am. I know Holly wants to be your friend, too."

Skylar glanced over her shoulder and shot her a skeptical look.

"I suppose she told you all about how we're here because my own father doesn't want me." She crossed her arms over her chest. Her eyes glistened with tears. "He doesn't want me. And I don't want him either. Today, I get to let him know that. If he even bothers to show up."

"Oh, Skylar." His tone was sympathetic. "No, Holly didn't tell me that. I'm really sorry you're going through such a rough time."

She looked at him warily. "She really didn't tell you?"

"She really didn't."

"I didn't." Holly gave her shoulder a squeeze. "I told you, you can trust me."

"No. I can't trust anyone." Skylar's eyes skittered down the hallway. Holly noted her looking at Alice and Shelley, who were deep in whispered conversation again. The mistrust in the teen's eyes was evident.

Sure, the girl had reason to doubt adults. But did she have a reason to doubt Alice, whom she'd lived with for several months now? Or Shelley, who had been her caseworker since she entered the system years ago?

"Skylar." Holly's tone was firm as the girl turned to look at her. "You can trust me. I promise. I have never given you a reason to doubt me. And while my situation is a bit up in the air at the moment, I will see what I can do about gaining custody of you when my life settles." She pulled in a breath. "I'm not promising anything because I don't make promises I can't keep. But I will do my best. That I can promise."

Skylar bit her lip as she stared into Holly's eyes. It was as if the teen were trying to see into Holly's soul, trying to see if she was trustworthy.

Suddenly Skylar nodded and threw her arms around Holly's waist.

Holly squeezed her tightly. Her heart ached for this girl, almost an adult, but still a child who needed and craved love and attention.

"Skylar." Shelley's voice was quiet but commanding as she strode toward them. "We need to go in now." The caseworker looked at Holly with raised eyebrows, as if wondering what they had been discussing.

Holly wasn't about to tell her. She trusted Shelley had Skylar's best interest at heart. Yet she wasn't about to betray Skylar's trust. Something was going on with the teen, something bigger and scarier than usual. While Shelley could possibly help with the issue, until Skylar completely confided in her, and convinced her Shelley wasn't part of the problem, she'd remain quiet.

"Let's go in." She disentangled the girl's arms from her waist. She took her hand instead. She gave it a squeeze and breathed a tiny sigh of relief when Skylar didn't pull away. She led the girl toward the courtroom, sparing a glance over her shoulder at Seth.

He was watching her with a furrowed brow as if he, too, suspected something foul was occurring.

They entered the courtroom where Judge Allen Cromwell sat on the bench, the raised platform at the front of the room.

"Good to see you again, Holly." The judge gave her a warm smile.

"You, too, Your Honor." She knew him from her time as a CASA as well as from her work with the police department. A few of the cases had gone to trial, and Holly had needed to testify. She had always found the judge to be personable and fair.

He greeted Shelley, then Skylar.

Skylar feigned a polite smile, then, still clutching her hand tightly, took a seat next to Holly.

She needed to put Skylar's strange behavior out of her mind and concentrate on being the advocate she'd signed up to be.

* * *

Seth couldn't help but feel anxious as he waited for Holly. A heavy feeling had settled into his chest as he thought about Skylar. There were so many children out there who should be loved and cherished but were not. He wondered if Skylar was a churchgoer and would add the girl to his prayer list.

He wanted to ask her about the car that had spooked her, then had tried to bomb the ranch, but he hadn't gotten the chance before she was whisked away.

The hearing seemed to be taking forever. This time of year, darkness fell early. He wasn't happy to be without his Mag. While Montana gun laws were fairly lenient, they still did not allow for a weapon to be brought into the courthouse or even the parking lot. With all the security measures, he felt they were safe enough in the building, but he was anxious to get Holly back to the ranch.

After what seemed like hours, Holly emerged with Skylar by her side. He couldn't tell by their expressions if it had gone well. Despite the earlier hug, Skylar looked withdrawn again. Seth kept his distance, allowing them privacy.

They said their goodbyes, and Skylar began walking to the entrance with Alice. Holly headed his way. She missed the longing look Skylar slid over her shoulder as she walked out the door.

Holly was right. Something was definitely troubling that kid. His heart went out to her. He wished he could do something to help, but if she wouldn't accept help from Holly, she was even less likely to accept it from him. Not that he had a clue what he could do for her. He was once again grateful for the supportive family he had. They'd always been there for him.

"Did you have a chance to ask her about the car?"

Holly winced. "I didn't. I'll call her later."

"We should get going. It'll be dark out soon."

Seth guided Holly out to the parking lot. It was almost devoid of cars as Skylar's case had been the last one of the day. He scoured the area, looking for the black car or any vehicle that seemed concerning.

A man strode toward them purposefully. Seth stiffened.

"That's the judge," Holly said under her breath.

Seth realized then that the man wasn't striding toward them but rather toward a dark SUV parked near the truck Seth had borrowed from his dad. It had seemed more prudent to take the four-wheel drive vehicle than Holly's car since the weather had caused the roads to become a bit treacherous.

The judge smiled when he caught sight of them.

"Hello, again, Judge."

"Holly, it's such a nice thing you do for these girls. They're fortunate to have you."

"Thank you. I hope you enjoy your evening."

"You, too. I heard you've had some trouble lately." Judge Cromwell paused, as if reading her surprised expression. "It's a small town. News travels. Stay safe."

"She will." Seth opened the passenger door for Holly and waited for her to slide inside. The judge got in his vehicle and drove away. Alice and Skylar were long gone, and it seemed that even Shelley had left. He jogged around the side of the vehicle, anxious to get back to the ranch.

When he slid into the driver's seat, he realized Holly was on the phone. He started up the truck, and she wrapped up the call as he was pulling out of the lot.

"That was Mateo." She slid her phone into her purse.

"He has some new information and asked if we could stop by the station before heading back to the ranch."

Fifteen minutes later they were seated in Mateo's office again.

"We finally got in touch with Todd Krause," he said. "He hasn't heard from Teresa in nearly a week, though he said that wasn't unusual. They speak often, just not daily. He tried to get a hold of her after we spoke to him but got no response. That concerned him. He drove to Mulberry Creek and met us at her house. The fact that he couldn't get a hold of her, and that the neighbors said she's been gone a few days, was enough to cause him concern. I'm happy he's been very cooperative. He was able to access her computer and look through her emails but didn't find anything suspicious. He went through her files and gave us her client list."

"Client list?" Seth leaned forward in his chair.

"She owns a small cleaning business that concentrates on commercial properties," Mateo said.

"There's been no sign of her at all?"

"No, Holly." Mateo frowned. "What we don't know is whether or not she took off willingly or if someone got to her."

Holly shuddered, fearing the worst. "They've come after me so relentlessly. I'm worried they went after her as well."

Mateo didn't seem to want to argue that point. "She's got a full roster of clients. We've made our way through the list. She hasn't gone to work the last several days, and the clients who were scheduled said that was very unlike her."

"No one reported her missing?" Seth's brows furrowed.

"A few of her clients were more put out by the fact

that their offices weren't cleaned than by the fact that a woman could possibly be missing. The other two thought it strange, but assumed something had come up."

Mateo slid a piece of paper toward her. "This is her list of clients. All the businesses are in Mulberry Creek, and all are on the smaller side, probably because she's a one-woman operation. I'm not sure if having a list of businesses will help with figuring out that ledger, but I thought it couldn't hurt."

"Thank you." Holly took the paper and skimmed down the list. She recognized most of the two dozen or so business names, and a handful of the owners.

"Todd admitted his mother had been distracted lately and seemed tense, nervous. However, she's been struggling with some health issues. He attributed her change in demeanor to that. He also admitted you did some work for him, which we knew. I asked if he recommended you to his mother." Mateo tapped his pen against his notepad, glancing over what he'd written. "He said he hadn't talked to her about it recently, but she was aware that he was pleased with your services."

Seth turned to Holly. "That's how she knew about you."

"That's the link," she agreed.

Mateo glanced at the clock on the wall. "It's been a long day. I won't keep you any longer. I mostly wanted to give you a copy of her clients, in case they held any relevance."

Mateo stood and they followed suit, all making promises to be in touch if anything came up.

"I feel so bad for her son," Holly said once they were back in the truck. "He must be frantic, worrying about his mother."

"I'm sure he is." Seth glanced at his phone. "I have a

text message from Mom. She said Chloe's having a great time with Wyatt. The two of them requested homemade burgers and fries for dinner. I'll let her know we're on our way."

"That sounds fabulous. I'm starving. But wait, would it be okay if we stopped to talk to Skylar? I want to ask her about the car. I could call her, though I'm afraid she won't answer. Since we're already in town it'll only take a few minutes."

"Sure." Seth was anxious for answers as well. "My cell battery is almost dead. Can you see if Dad has a charger in here?"

Holly found a charger in the glove box. She got Seth's phone situated as he drove to Alice and Skylar's.

"Was it my imagination," Seth began as he drove, "or was there some major tension in the air between the social worker and the foster mom?"

"Yes," Holly said, "I felt that as well. I wish I knew what they were talking about. If it had to do with Skylar, it's probably something I should be aware of, yet neither was willing to share."

"Any idea what kind of car either drives?"

"What?" Holly's surprise was clear. "You're wondering about the sporty car? It couldn't have been Alice. She was inside the house when the car drove by. I'm not sure about Shelley. But I don't think she could afford a car like that on a social worker's salary. Besides, why would either of them ever want to blow up the ranch?"

Seth arched a brow. "Why would anyone?"

They pulled up to the curb, cutting off further discussion. The lights blazed from within, making the house look warm and inviting.

"I'll wait here." Seth preempted Holly's request.

"Thank you. I'll be as fast as I can."

* * *

The conversation had gone even quicker than Holly had imagined. Alice had let her in willingly enough, but Skylar had clammed up immediately. When asked about the black car she'd crossed her arms and lifted her chin defiantly. She had the nerve to pretend she hadn't seen a black car. She acted as if she had no idea what Holly was talking about.

Her blatant fibbing only increased Holly's concern.

"Why would she lie if she had nothing to hide?" Holly asked Seth as they finally headed toward the ranch. "She obviously *is* lying, which tells me she clearly *is* hiding something."

Holly pressed two fingers to her temple and rubbed.

When it had become clear that Skylar wasn't going to talk, Holly told her about the car coming to the ranch. Told her about the drone and the bomb. She hated to scare the teen, who was already obviously scared enough, but she'd hoped it would be enough to shake a confession out of the girl. Instead, Skylar had raced from the kitchen, where they'd been talking, and run straight to her room, slamming the door.

Alice had told Holly, quite firmly, that she didn't think Holly's presence was helping Skylar. She had gone so far as to suggest she relinquish her CASA duties. There was no way Holly was going to abandon the teen now.

Sleet had started to come down again, coating the windshield. Seth turned the wipers on and slowed the truck a bit.

"I don't like that Alice asked you to stop being her CASA. Not after what I saw between her and Shelley today. I picked up on the wary way Skylar eyed the two of them. How well do you know them?"

Before Holly could answer, Seth cut in again.

"I hate to say this, but I think we have company."

Holly corkscrewed her neck. Dread sizzled through her at the note of warning in Seth's tone. They had rounded a curve, and, seemingly from nowhere, a vehicle had sneaked up behind them. The headlights sliced through the darkness. She let out an involuntary shriek as the vehicle slammed into their back bumper.

"Hold on!" Seth shouted.

Then the vehicle rammed into them again.

TEN

They twisted, fishtailed on the slick road, then slid sideways across the shoulder, through the ditch and into the tree line. The back passenger door took the brunt of the impact. They were jolted hard, their seat belts the only thing keeping them from injury.

"Are you okay, Holly?"

"I think so."

Headlights sliced through the cab of the truck. Holly's eyes widened in terror.

"They're coming!" She unbuckled their seat belts hurriedly and then yanked the door handle open, and with more strength than Seth would've thought possible for her small frame, she tugged him across the seat of the truck before he fully realized what was happening. She scrambled out the door, and he tumbled out after her.

As they took off running, he heard a sickening crunch. He glanced over his shoulder. The Bronco had floored its gas pedal and hit the driver's door head-on. If not for Holly's quick thinking he would've been crushed.

The vehicle backed up again. Seth wasn't sure if the attackers realized they'd gotten out of the vehicle. He wasn't going to stick around to find out. A moment later, the headlights swept through the woods, washing over him and Holly.

He knew they'd been spotted.

"Cut to the left." He realized the trajectory would be difficult for the vehicle's headlights to track. She did so immediately, and the two of them ran as if their lives depended on it, because, of course, they both knew full well that they did.

It was dark, sleeting, and the wind was fierce.

The Bronco's doors slammed.

He heard men shouting and knew they were being pursued on foot.

"Keep moving, Holly. We have a head start, and I don't want to lose it."

They wove around trees, nearly stumbled over fallen logs, had their faces slapped by stray, stinging branches. Still, they pressed on. He was grateful the men didn't seem to have flashlights. Apparently it hadn't occurred to them that running the truck off the road might not be enough.

The boom of a gunshot split the air. Then another.

The men must be blindly shooting, hoping to hit one of their targets.

Or perhaps hoping to scare them into giving themselves away.

Holly gasped but didn't cry out, which Seth remembered was how she'd given herself away that first night. He heard her whimper, and he knew her fear. They were being hunted. His anger surged. He was furious that someone was doing this to Holly. Chasing her. Terrorizing her. Trying to kill her.

He hated that he felt so helpless and vowed he would not be without a weapon again.

Please, God, help me to keep her safe.

She was such a good person. A loving mother to Chloe, a pillar of support for foster girls, a cat rescuer.

Squinting against the sleet biting into his face, he was able to make out an odd shape up ahead. It was jaggedly rounded and roughly the size of his dining room table. He'd spent enough time in the woods to realize it was a tree that had blown over in a storm. It had pulled a good chunk of earth up with its roots.

Without saying a word he grabbed Holly's arm. She glanced over her shoulder, slowing. Silently, he pulled her toward the tree. They couldn't keep up this pace. Blindly running into the forest in this awful weather in the dark could prove to be every bit as deadly as the men chasing them.

She realized immediately what his intention was, and she darted behind the uprooted tree with him, taking refuge behind the makeshift shield. They hunched down, making themselves smaller, and tried to catch their breaths.

He pressed a finger to her lips as she'd done to him the other day when she'd spotted Briar pacing. She nodded in understanding.

They sat there in the darkness.

Listening.

Waiting.

Watching.

Minutes ticked by slowly.

If Seth had to, he'd take on the men weaponless. He was trained in hand-to-hand combat, but he hoped it wouldn't come to that.

He continued to peer into the darkness, ears straining for any whisper of noise. But all he heard was his and Holly's labored breathing. He didn't see anything.

No movement. No questionable shadows. Certainly no telling beam of a flashlight.

"I think we lost them," he murmured.

"Thank You, Lord," Holly whispered. "Thank You for protecting us."

"Keep praying, because we aren't out of this yet. Do you happen to have your cell phone?"

He felt Holly reach toward her pocket. Then she let out a frustrated huff. "I don't. It's in my purse. My purse in the truck. You don't have yours?"

"No," he said grimly. "I had it charging. Remember? It's in the truck, too."

"We need to get back to the vehicle."

"We can't," Seth told her. "I don't think they planned on chasing us through the woods. I doubt they know the area any better than I do. My guess is they headed back. They probably assume we will, too."

"They'll be waiting for us," Holly realized.

"I think it's probable." Seth glanced around. Trying to get his bearings. "The good news is the sleet has let up."

"The bad news is that we're already wet. I'm sure glad I didn't wear a dress to the hearing. I'm also grateful I have decent shoes on and not high heels."

He'd barely noticed the cold when they'd been barreling through the woods, but now that they'd slowed, he could feel the chill setting in. The fact that they were both wet with no way to warm up in these frigid temps could become potentially life-threatening.

"True. We need to get moving. It'll help us to stay warm."

"If we're not going back to the truck, where are we going?"

He caught what he thought, hoped, was a sliver of

moonlight. He tried picturing the moon as he'd last noticed it from the road. It had been to their left, to the east.

"Come on." He grabbed her hand and stood, pulling
her to her feet as well. He was going on instinct, but it
was all he had right now. "I think if we head this way,
we'll be parallel to the road." He didn't want to cut back
directly to the vehicle, but he did want to return to some
type of civilization. He hoped they could loop around the
way they'd come, yet come out farther down the road,
where the men would not likely be waiting.

Holly's stomach growled so loudly it seemed to echo
in the silence.

"Sorry," she murmured. "I'm starving. I want to go
home to my daughter and eat one of those cheeseburgers your mom mentioned. I bet the fries are crispy and
salty and perfect. I've never wanted a burger so badly
in my life."

His lips quirked, despite the severity of the situation.
"I couldn't agree more. I don't think they're lurking in
the woods, but we need to be as quiet as possible, just
in case."

"Agreed," she whispered.

Her stomach roared again.

He eased out from behind the tree roots, and she followed.

Please, God, please let me be on the right path.

He'd always had a good sense of direction, but he
knew how easy it was to get turned around. Even sea-
soned hikers got lost sometimes. With this foray into the
woods at breakneck speed being unplanned, the condi-
tions were far from ideal.

They walked.

And walked.

When he thought he couldn't stand the heartbreaking

sound of Holly's teeth chattering one moment longer, they eased into a clearing.

Disappointment slammed into him.

A clearing? He had been hoping for a road.

Even as they trekked, he'd been hyperaware of his surroundings. Not only had he listened for their attackers, but he'd listened for the hum of engines. He'd watched for the hint of headlights glinting in the distance but had been disappointed.

Only the sounds of branches breaking beneath their feet and the clatter of Holly's teeth had broken the silence.

Somewhere along the way, he'd almost tripped over a chunk of debris. When he'd realized it was a stubby but sturdy branch that could suffice as a makeshift club, he'd grabbed it. It was no match for a gun, but it was surely better than nothing.

He fought down a frustrated growl.

Now what? He was freezing, and Holly clearly was, too. And now they were lost.

"What's that?" Holly nudged him.

He turned to her, surprised by the hope in her tone.

"What?" His gaze skimmed the darkness.

She pointed. "Up there."

It took him a moment to focus, pinpoint what she'd somehow spotted. When he did, his own hope sparked.

"It's a deer stand. For hunting." He knew exactly what it was. It was a small structure the size of a child's tree house, but built on stilts. It overlooked the field they'd stumbled across. Seth had spent plenty of time in a similar stand, watching and waiting patiently for deer to wander onto the clearing.

"Come on."

Holly took off, and he hustled after her.

She, too, seemed to realize they were not on track to

find the road because there should have been some sign of it by now.

A wooden ladder was built into the structure. At the top of the ladder was a small platform, and, in the darkness, Seth could make out the white door that led inside.

"I hope it's open. Please, let it be open."

He hoped so, too. It wouldn't be unheard of. It wasn't as if people left anything of value inside. Stands were simply an elevated place to sit, out of the elements, during hunting season. Regardless, if it was locked, he'd have no qualms about breaking in. He'd make up for the damages later.

She scurried up the ladder, and he stayed on the ground, scanning the area, though he was almost certain they were not being followed.

Holly's relieved voice cut into the silence. "It's open."

He glanced up in time to see her slip inside. He hurried up the ladder after her. Once he was inside, he closed the door.

The space was dark.

Small. Half the size of his walk-in closet.

"I'm warmer already."

"Really?" Seth hadn't noticed a difference in temp. He'd thought it was as cold inside as out.

"There's no wind in here. And it's dry. Two things I'm grateful for." She heaved out a weary sigh. "I hope there aren't any rodents in here. I need to sit."

Seth heard her drop to the floor. Despite their situation, he couldn't help but smile. He had never known anyone as upbeat as Holly. He was ready to grumble about the cold, and here she was grateful to be out of the wind and happy to have a place to sit.

"On the bright side," Holly continued, and his lips twitched again.

"There's a bright side?" he teased as he lowered himself onto the planked floor next to her.

"Several, actually. We didn't die, for one," she teased back. "But seriously, I think the wind dried my coat."

"Huh." He realized she was right. "Are you always so positive?"

"I try to be. What's the point in grumbling? None."

"True enough." He decided to look for the bright side himself. "Now we at least have shelter until our rescue party comes."

He couldn't make her out in the dark, but he could envision her tipping her head curiously to the side.

"You think there will be a rescue party?"

"Absolutely." He was certain. "As soon as Mom realizes we aren't home when we should be, she'll have half the county out looking for us. Considering what's been happening, I'm guessing Detective Bianchi will have half the force out searching, too."

What he didn't mention was that because they'd gone to see Skylar, who lived on the other side of Mulberry Creek, he'd taken a roundabout way back to the ranch. The route had been shorter than backtracking all the way through town, but would anyone think to look for them on these back roads?

"You're so blessed," Holly said quietly, "to have the family that you have. You all are so close."

He couldn't miss the note of longing in her voice. When they were younger he'd thought it was sad that her mom had run off, leaving Holly behind and not once checking in on her. It was crummy that she was stuck with a dad who was kind of a jerk. But he'd never really thought about what that meant. He hadn't considered what it was to miss the support and love that came with a tight-knit family.

"If I went missing on my own," she continued wistfully, "I wonder how long it would take someone to notice. If I had a family like yours, I'd never be able to pick up my life, move to Bozeman and leave them behind."

He knew she was referring to his impending move. In that moment, it was hard to disagree with her.

"Sorry, that was rude. It's your life. Of course you should live it how you want," she said with feeling. "I'm happy you found something you'll be passionate about."

"Thanks for that." But the question was…what did he want? He had been so sure of his future before running into Holly. Now his carefully thought-out plans suddenly didn't seem to make sense. He wished Holly didn't sound so cheery about it, and he hoped she'd hint that she wanted him to stay. Ironic, since the same words from Eric grated on his nerves, yet he longed to hear Holly ask him.

Holly cringed, wishing she could see Seth's expression in the darkness. All she could make out was a vague outline of his body. She had no right to nudge her nose into his business. No right to comment on his life at all. No one did. He had said as much to his brother, and she needed to respect that. To make up for it, she tried to backtrack and correct her mistake.

"Not only was it rude, it was wrong. I think it's great that you're following your heart and chasing your dreams." Even though she found herself wishing he would stay, the words were true. He *should* follow his heart. Seth was a great guy, and he deserved to be happy. "I hope helping me isn't interfering too much with your plans. I'd hate to know I kept you in Mulberry Creek longer than necessary."

She felt him shift next to her as if the statement made him uncomfortable.

"Nope. You're not keeping me. I'd planned on staying here through the winter."

"That's good." Her tone was upbeat, but her heart ached with sadness. "What made you decide to join your friend in his business?"

"I guess I haven't been happy at the ranch for quite some time. I wanted a change. Tucker is a military buddy I've kept in touch with. When I saw him a while ago, he mentioned his uncle was retiring and he'd be looking for a new partner."

"That's great." She knew her answer sounded lame, but it was difficult to scrounge up enthusiasm when the knowledge that he was leaving made her feel so glum.

"Speaking of chasing dreams, how is that you ended up going to college? If I recall, that wasn't in your future. If you don't mind me asking."

Did she mind?

She wasn't sure how to answer that question without ripping open their entire history.

She hadn't been entirely honest with him years ago.

Could she do it now?

Tell him everything?

Or close to it?

"I don't mind." Where did she begin, though? "I wanted to go to college and knew I had to find a way to make it happen. My grades were good enough, I managed to get scholarships and qualified for some financial aid. That paid for most of my schooling, but housing was another matter. One day I was searching for places to rent in Missoula. They were all so far out of my price range, and I saw an ad placed by an older woman. She was offering free room and board in exchange for light housekeeping, grocery shopping and the occasional ride somewhere. She had a car, though she couldn't drive anymore due to advanced macular degeneration. I answered the ad. Vivienne and I hit it off right away. One of the tasks she was adamant about was that her boarder needed to drive her to church every Sunday and to her Bible study on Thursday afternoons. It didn't take much nudging for her to convince me to go to both with her, instead of simply providing the transportation."

"Is she...?" Seth let the unfinished question hang in the air.

"She's alive and well and still full of spunk." Holly smiled affectionately. "She's moved into an assisted living facility now. She's become a surrogate grandmother to Chloe. We make the hour drive and go visit her every other Sunday. She's been such a blessing to me. I've called her Aunt Viv for years. She's like family. I stayed with her all through college, including my master's program."

"Tell me more about your dad." Seth's tone was careful but curious. "I know you didn't get along the best, but were things really that bad? So bad you had to leave town?"

Holly blew out a sigh. Maybe it was time, all these years later, to tell Seth the truth about what she'd endured growing up.

"I didn't have the best home life, Seth. After my mom took off, my dad drank. A lot. I think I hinted at that."

"You did," he said quietly, "but I think I was too naive at the time to comprehend how that could really affect you."

"He was a mean drunk." Holly cringed at the memory. "He was verbally abusive. He would say the most awful things to me. He blamed me for Mom leaving. He said if I was a better kid, more lovable, she would've stayed."

She hesitated as memories she'd sealed away began to work free. She squeezed her eyes shut and leaned her head back, grateful for the darkness so Seth couldn't see the misery on her face.

"Why didn't you ever tell me?"

"I was young, embarrassed. You had this great family and seemingly perfect life. He always told me I was trash, not worthy of you. He would say that you were only with me because you felt sorry for me." She had worked hard to overcome her past, the fears, hurts and misconceptions about herself. Talking about it now dredged up pain she thought she'd gotten over. "I thought if I told you about it, and you stayed with me, that he would be right. I worried you would feel sorry for me. I also feared the opposite would happen, that you would realize he was right and that I was trash, like he said, and leave."

Seth grabbed her hand and gripped it hard. "Never."

"I've come a long way since those days." Holly relished how her hand felt in his. It was still chilled, but their two hands together created warmth. It seemed to float up her arm and wrap around her heart. "Mostly thanks to Aunt Viv. She brought me to Christ, and my life has never been the same."

Don't ever question your worth, Holly, Aunt Vivienne would say. *You belong to the King of Kings. You are absolutely priceless. You are so precious to Him that He died for you. Don't ever forget the depth of His love.*

"It's because of Vivienne that I decided to become a foster parent," Holly continued. "I wasn't in foster care but maybe I should have been. I wanted to help girls who were struggling like I was. I got licensed with the intention of taking in teens. God had other plans. The first call I received was asking if I'd take a toddler. I had no experience with small children. I couldn't say no, though. The foster family she'd been with for nearly a year had recently found out their biological child had a heart condition. Suddenly their world was turned upside down, filled with doctor's visits and trying to cope with the news. Chloe's biological mom had been working toward reunification. The social worker told me she thought Chloe would be back with her mom within three months at the most."

"What happened?" Seth was still holding her hand. His thumb swirled against her skin, the touch soft and encouraging.

"I met the woman several times because she had visitation with Chloe. It was clear she loved her daughter. I was rooting for her, praying for her, hoping she would straighten her life out so she could gain custody again. Unfortunately, she was fighting a drug addiction. She seemed to be doing so well. And then…"

"Then?"

"She overdosed." Holly's tone conveyed her sadness. "Suddenly, this child that I adored, but that I was prepared to give up so she could be with her mother, became an orphan. She had no other family. From the moment I received the news, I knew I would do whatever I had to do to make her my daughter. As it turned out, the process went smoothly because she was already living with me. Chloe has officially been mine for nearly two years now."

"God put her right where she needed to be. You are an amazing mother."

"That is one of the kindest things anyone has ever said to me." Seth's words settled into her soul. "Vivienne instilled in me the importance of faith and family. I didn't have that frame of reference growing up."

She shifted to face him. The clouds were starting to clear, and though it was still dark, she could easily make out his silhouette. She could tell he was facing her as well.

"Seth, I need you to know how sorry I am about Ella. When I left town all those years ago, I didn't have a cell phone. I didn't have any social media accounts. I wasn't exactly hiding from my dad, but I didn't want to make it easy for him to find me, either. That was probably unnecessary since I don't know if he would've even tried. Regardless, I was in a bad place, and I needed a fresh start. A clean slate. Only I think I kept the slate a little too clean." She squeezed his hand. "I didn't hear of her passing until she'd been gone over a year. I ran into a mutual friend of ours, and he mentioned it. I tried to reach out to you, but I found out you had joined the Marines. You were deployed, so I let it go." She squinted into the darkness, now wishing she could see his face. "I didn't even know you were interested in the Marines."

He cleared his throat. "Losing Ella was tough on the family. Eric went off the rails for a while. With Ella being his twin, he really struggled. He's cleaned up his life now, but a few years were rough. My parents were so lost in their grief, but at least they had each other. Nina's always had a strong faith. She really leaned into her friends, mostly girls from her church youth group. I was grieving but felt I was on my own. I knew I needed some kind of structure, something to keep me in line because I didn't want to end up like Eric." She felt him shrug. "I decided joining the military was the answer. I was floundering, and I needed purpose."

"I'm sorry," she whispered. She was sorry for leaving him, sorry for the fact that he felt alone when he was surrounded by so many people. "I wish I'd been there for you."

She cringed as she realized what she said. The words were out of her mouth, and like a spilled can of soda, there was no way to put them back.

He asked the question she had been waiting for.

"Why weren't you?"

"I ended things with you and I left town because I felt that I didn't deserve you. After listening to my father year after year, tearing me down, berating me, it was hard not to believe he was right. You were a great guy, with a great family and a promising future. You were planning on going to school for agricultural science. You had a plan. I didn't see myself going anywhere after high school. Not unless I left town. I thought you could do so much better than me."

"Holly, no—"

"You have no idea what it's like to be a young, impressionable teenager and have someone close to you, someone who should love and support you, treat you that way." She felt now, after all these years, she owed him the honesty that she hadn't given him back then. "It is terrible to be told that no one wants you. To be told daily that you're a mistake. That your own mother didn't love you. Seth, the emotional wounds his words caused, they took a toll on me. Looking back, I think he was so miserable, and he saw I was happy, and he wanted to destroy it. He succeeded."

"None of what he said was true. You were amazing. Then and now. Smart. Caring. Genuine. He was wrong to say no one wanted you." He leaned toward her, pressing his forehead against hers. "*I* wanted you. *I* loved you. We may have been young, but I wanted you with my whole heart."

The emotion in his words wrapped around her. She

wanted to sink into them as she remembered the innocent but all-consuming love they had shared.

"That's why when I left, I wrote you a letter. In my own messed-up way, I thought I was doing what was best for you. I thought I was setting you free. I was afraid if I broke up with you in person, you would talk me out of it," she admitted.

Now he was the one leaving. They couldn't go down this path again because there was no point. Yet being here with him, it was so hard not to love him as she had back then. But he was moving to the other side of the state. What was she going to do? Follow him? Quit her job? Uproot Chloe? Uproot their lives on a chance, on a hope, that maybe she and Seth had a future? She couldn't do that. Chloe needed consistency. Holly needed a steady job. Their friends, their church, their support system was in Mulberry Creek. Getting over Seth once had been excruciating, almost impossible. She wouldn't allow herself to fall in love again, only to have to go through that all over again. Best to not let those feelings flourish in the first place.

She tilted her face toward his, ever so slightly. It was enough. Their lips met. The kiss was short, sweet, but seemed to hold years of stored-up emotions and longing.

"What was that for?" he whispered.

Was that hope she heard in his voice? Or confusion?

Why had she kissed him? She had no business giving in to her feelings. This situation was complicated enough. He was leaving, and he owed her nothing. She had already sent his life into a tailspin once before. It would not be fair to repay his recent kindness by doing that to him again.

"That," she said quietly as her heart broke a little, "was for the closure we never had back then."

Closure? The moment the word slipped from her mouth she knew it was a lie. Kissing Seth did not provide closure. If anything, it caused her love for him to overflow all the more.

ELEVEN

Seth's head snapped up. He blinked into the darkness, taking only a moment to orient himself and remember where they were. His memories from last night snapped into place and his heart lurched.

Holly had kissed him.

For *closure*.

She had shared things with him she had never shared before. He felt closer to her than ever. Never had he disclosed to anyone the real reason he'd joined the Marines. Yet last night he'd told her. Just when he dared to hope that there was a chance for them, she had shut him down.

It was a blow to his heart.

A good reminder that he and Holly were not meant to be.

Yet his memories were not what had awakened him.

What, then?

In the moonlight he could see Holly was still nestled beside him, scrunched up, sound asleep. Her legs were stretched out, and her head leaned against the wall. The clouds had dissipated, and the sky was dappled with dazzling stars. It was a sight he'd appreciate most any other night.

But not now, as his mind scrambled to reorient itself.

He was cold. So unbelievably, deep-down-into-his-bones cold. But he was awake, alive, and obviously he hadn't frozen to death. So there was that.

Was it the chill that had awakened him?

Or was it something else?

Someone?

As he was about to clamber to his feet to look out the windows of the deer stand, he heard a sound.

A dog barking.

It sounded distant, but several heartbeats later it barked again, closer this time.

He leaped up. His bones seemed to creak and scream in protest from having been in an uncomfortable, cramped position for so long.

"Holly!" He gave her nudge. "Wake up."

He couldn't see her very well in the darkness, but he felt her become instantly alert. Another round of barking sounded.

"What's that?"

He clasped her hand and tugged her to her feet.

She groaned as she fought the same stiff muscles he'd struggled with.

"A dog." He knew that wasn't her real question. "I'm not sure if it's friend or foe."

Had their pursuers found a new way to track them?

Were they safer in the deer stand than on the ground?

Yes.

Maybe.

The door didn't lock. There was nothing but his own body to use for a barricade, which he would do if it came to that.

On the ground, the dog would track them for sure. And if the dog wasn't friendly, well, they'd have a real problem. Besides, there was no way they'd have time to descend the ladder and make a run for it. As they'd learned last night, there was nowhere to go anyway.

"I see lights." Holly gripped his arm. "They're headed this way."

He had noticed them as well. Flashlights. Three distinct beams.

A search party, for sure.

But who was heading it?

Law enforcement?

Or a pack of killers?

His heart thumped fast and hard as his mind spun with theories.

Once again, he longed for his Mag. There was nothing he could do about that. He gripped the solid tree limb that he'd confiscated from the forest floor the night before, willing to use it like a club if he had to. It was better than nothing, and he'd had to make do before.

Movement below caught his attention. The dog burst from the clearing, then let out a cacophony of barking so loud Seth thought they could probably hear the animal all the way back in Mulberry Creek. A moment later a flashlight beam swept over the dog.

He was hit with a jolt of recognition.

And relief. Such intense relief.

"That looks like a SAR dog," he muttered. The gratitude he felt was so thick he could have collapsed under it.

"A what?" Holly's confused tone implied she wasn't sure if that was a good or bad thing.

"A search and rescue dog. See the vest it's wearing?"

A moment later a uniformed officer jogged onto the field after the dog. Then another.

And another.

"They found us." Holly threw her arms around Seth

and squeezed. Ignoring the ache in his side, he squeezed her back. "We're going to be okay."

"Thank You, Lord." Seth closed his eyes and felt his thankfulness in every cell of his body. And thank-you to his family, for surely, they had contacted Mateo the moment they realized Holly and Seth weren't home when they should be. God had blessed him with such an amazing support system. He'd always known it. His conversation with Holly last night had jacked his appreciation of them up to a whole new level.

"You were right." Holly's voice trembled as she stepped away. "They came for us. We're going to go home."

Seth opened the door of the deer stand and called a greeting to the rescue crew.

"Looking for us?"

The trio let out a whoop in celebration at having found Seth and Holly unscathed.

The next few minutes felt chaotic as the handler ordered the exuberant dog back and gave her what appeared to be a favorite toy to play with.

Another officer called in Seth and Holly's location.

One officer offered them hot coffee from a thermos, which they gladly gulped down. The same man also produced heated mittens and two hats from the pack he carried. The heated mittens felt amazing. The coffee seemed to warm them from the inside out.

Seth was anxious to get home even though the elements now seemed a bit more tolerable.

He realized the officer calling in their location was his old buddy, Joe Rollins, the officer who had shared his cruiser earlier in the week while pulling night watch at Holly's. When Joe got off the call, Seth held out a hand.

"Thanks for finding us."

"You can thank Scout." Joe nodded at the spaniel.

"Took us a while to find your vehicle. We've been look-ing all over the county through the night. Once we found the truck, called in Scout and put her on your scent, she led us straight to you."

"Impressive." Holly eyed the dog with admiration.

"I spoke with Detective Bianchi. He's been in contact with your family since the start of this. He's back at the crash site, processing the scene. He'll give your family a call. It goes without saying they've been pretty wor-ried." Joe turned to Holly. "Is there anyone we can con-tact on your behalf?"

"No," Holly said and left it at that.

Seth heard the sadness in her voice.

Holly had no one. Well, she did have her Aunt Viv, but she was safely ensconced in her assisted living facil-ity and wouldn't even have known Holly was missing.

He slipped his arm around her shoulder without think-ing. It felt like the right thing to do. It must have been because she leaned into him, sighing as she rested her head on his shoulder.

"It'll be daylight soon. Think you can walk out of here?" Joe's assessing gaze scanned over them. "Or we could try to get some ATVs back here for you."

"We can make it out." Holly's head snapped up. "I'm anxious to get back."

"I can imagine," Joe said.

The jolt of caffeine and the relief over being rescued had given Seth renewed energy. He assumed Holly felt the same.

"Yeah, we can make it out of here. As long as you can lead the way."

When they arrived back at the ranch, they were greeted by Seth's loving family. The scent of cheeseburgers and fries, Holly's craving from the night before, hung in the air. When Seth had mentioned to Julia that they were starving because they'd missed the dinner they'd badly wanted, she had made sure to have it prepared for them, despite the odd hour. Chloe wasn't up, but after hugs all around from the rest of the crew, Holly couldn't stop herself from checking in on her daughter before satisfying her appetite.

Chloe was fast asleep on the futon in Seth's office, cuddling her pink knitted blanket. Briar was curled up next to her. Neither feline nor child stirred as Holly poked her head inside, said a prayer of thanks for her safe homecoming then backed out the door. She was grateful Chloe had slept through the ordeal, not even realizing her momma was missing last night as Julia tucked her into bed.

Dawn was breaking, and Holly could hear Seth's family chattering in the kitchen. She thought she should probably be tired after their ordeal, but she'd slept some in the deer stand and was now oddly wide-awake.

They had given Mateo what few details they could about the vehicle that ran them off the road. When the truck had spun around after being hit, the headlights sliced across the night, briefly highlighting a dark green vehicle that Seth was fairly certain was a Bronco. It had happened so fast, then they'd hit the tree and gone on the run.

"How are you doing?"

Holly whirled at the sound of Seth's soft voice.

"Sorry. I didn't mean to startle you. We didn't want to start breakfast without you." He grinned. "If you can call cheeseburgers and fries breakfast."

"Your mom is amazing." Holly smiled back. "A burger has never sounded so good."

"Mommy?" Chloe's sleepy voice drifted to her from the other room.

Holly glanced over her shoulder to see Chloe trudging toward her. She wiped her eyes with one hand and still clutched her blanket with the other.

"Hey, baby." She knelt and scooped her daughter into her arms. A feeling of intense love coursed through her as she held her tight, relishing the sweetness of the moment.

"I missed you last night."

"I missed you, too." Holly squeezed her again.

"Seth, you're back, too." Chloe scrubbed at her sleepy eyes. "I missed my mom *and* you."

"I'm back now." He reached over and tousled her already messy hair.

Holly was surprised, and not at all disappointed, when Chloe leaned away from her, reaching for Seth.

He didn't hesitate in taking Chloe from Holly's arms. Chloe's arms squeezed around his neck, and he squeezed her back.

She giggled.

"You hug tight like my momma."

Seth chuckled. "You hug pretty tight, too, kiddo."

"Momma taught me how," Chloe declared as she finally released her grip around Seth's neck.

"I'm sure she did." Seth winked at Holly.

Chloe sniffed the air, her nose crinkled comically like a bunny rabbit's.

"I smell something yummy."

"That would probably be French fries," Seth said.

"Or the burgers," Holly added. "Are you hungry?"

"French fries for breakfast?" Chloe looked intrigued. Seth placed her on her feet, and she trotted off to the kitchen.

Seth chuckled as he watched her go. Then he turned to Holly and his expression grew serious.

His gaze held hers. She knew him well enough to know he wanted to say something. What else was there to say after last night? They were headed different directions in life.

He leaned in close. She could feel his breath drifting across her neck. She suspected he wanted to kiss her again. And she wanted him to. Oh, how she wanted Seth to kiss her. How she wanted to lose herself in her love for him.

"Holly." His voice was barely above a whisper, but her name seemed to hold so many questions. "I—"

She pressed a finger to his lips, sealing in whatever he was about to say.

"Your mom has breakfast ready. Everyone is waiting for us."

He took a step back as a frown slipped onto his face. "Right. We wouldn't want to keep everyone waiting."

With those words he turned and walked away.

Several hours later, after eating breakfast and watching one of Chloe's movies on the big-screen TV in the family room, Holly decided to take a nap. Yawning, Chloe agreed to join her. The moment they disappeared into Seth's office, he went in search of his parents. He found them in the kitchen. Julia was flipping through a cookbook. James was cutting himself a slice of freshly baked pumpkin bread.

He walked in, gave his dad a bear hug. Then promptly turned to his mother, who was seated at the table. He leaned over and gave her a quick hug, too.

"In case you didn't know, you two are the best." Before he could be overcome by emotion, he hustled out of the kitchen, leaving his parents to wonder what had just happened. Talking with Holly last night had made him realize anew how blessed he was to have such a loving family.

He knew he should try to get some rest but also knew that wouldn't be possible. He was exhausted from their ordeal the night before, yet was too wired to sleep.

Instead, he went out to the barn and was surprised to find Eric there. Even more surprised to realize his brother was cleaning out the horse stalls.

"What's going on here?" Seth smirked. "You don't have enough of your own work to do?"

Eric came out of Echo's stall and placed the pitchfork against the wall.

"You helped me out when I was going through a rough time last year. I thought it was only fair to return the favor."

Yes, he had a great family, for sure.

"Thanks, I appreciate it."

"You sure gave us a scare last night." Eric folded his arms and leaned against the stall. "Scared Mom to death. Me, too, if you want to know the truth."

"I'll admit, it was pretty nerve-wracking to be chased through the woods in the dark, knowing the men were armed." Seth frowned, his chest tightening at the memory. "Would have been bad enough if the men were just after me. Thinking they could get to Holly, that was tough."

He blew out a breath and tried to calm his racing heart. Imagining what could have happened sent chills through him.

"By the grace of God."

"You took the words right out of my mouth." Seth

raked a hand through his hair. "The thought of any harm coming to Holly? It's about more than I can take."

Eric leveled a knowing gaze on him. "You still have feelings for her."

"I'd be worried about anyone."

"Of course." Eric nodded. "But this isn't just anyone. It's Holly. I remember how head over heels you were for her. Now she's back, pretty and sweet as ever. Has a cute little girl to boot. I could see how old feelings would get fired up. If they ever fizzled in the first place."

"They fizzled." Seth heard the argument in his tone. "It's not like I've been pining for her all these years."

"Pining?"

"You know what I mean." Seth wasn't sure he wanted to have this conversation with Eric, though maybe he needed to talk to someone. "But seeing her again? Now I really understand the saying 'a blast from the past,' because that's exactly what it felt like. It's like getting hit with an explosion of memories and..."

"Feelings?" Eric arched a brow.

"Yeah. Lots of feelings," he grumbled. "The thing is, not all the feelings are good. That girl broke my heart. She shattered it."

"Seth, she was barely eighteen. Practically still a kid," Eric reminded him. "I'm sure you aren't proud of everything you did back then. I seem to recall a practical joke that involved the principal's office and a rooster that went terribly wrong."

"Point taken." And really, her explanation last night had reframed the entire breakup in his mind.

"How do you feel about her now?"

"That's just it, Eric. I'm having a hard time differentiating how I'm feeling now with how I felt back then.

How do I know if what I'm feeling now is legit, or if it's an echo of past feelings?"

"Can't it be both? You two have a history. Of course there's something there. I think it's worth looking into."

"She kissed me last night." Seth shrugged and hurried on before Eric could comment. "For closure. There's nothing to look into."

Eric frowned as if he didn't know what to say to that.

"You know what I could really use right now?"

"Name it."

"A nice ride around the ranch on Echo."

"That's not a bad idea." Eric pushed away from the corral. "Let me saddle up Rio and I'll join you. It wouldn't hurt to ride around the perimeter."

Seth was grateful for Eric's offer. He was even more grateful for it several hours later when they ended their ride. He hadn't realized how much he'd needed a breather. Being out on the ranch, soaking in the beauty of God's creation, had calmed his nerves and helped soothe his soul.

He was feeling refreshed rather than exhausted when he went inside to find Holly. He looked in the kitchen first, as that seemed to be the central gathering place. His mom and Chloe were working on some type of a craft at the table, and his dad was reading a book. Julia told him Holly was in his office, her makeshift guest room.

He found her there, with the door cracked open. She had tidied the room, had put the futon back in the sofa position, and was pacing the small space.

Back and forth. Back and forth. Today her typically tidy ponytail was traded in for a careless knot on top of her head. A pencil protruded from it. She wore a hoodie and yoga pants, and was in her stocking feet.

She gripped the ledger in one hand, while the fingers of her other massaged her temple.

He stood in the doorway, not wanting to lurk, but also feeling as if this was not a good time to interrupt.

Back and forth she went a few times more.

He was preparing to retreat when she gasped, and her hand flew to her mouth.

"Holly?" he asked, alarmed by her obvious distress. "What's wrong?"

Her hand dropped from her lips. She blinked at him, as if startled to see him, then spun and lunged for her phone. It had been resting on the arm of the futon.

Seth strode into the room and watched over her shoulder as she logged onto a social media site. She brought up the Mulberry Creek Police Department.

"Holly?" His tone was sharper this time.

Her movements seemed frantic as she ignored him, scrolling.

Finally, apparently having found what she was looking for, she glanced up. Then she swiveled back around to grab the ledger she'd placed on his desk.

She glanced at him, then at the ledger. She jabbed at the page.

"This column. I realized it's dates. In this country, we denote a date by month, day then year. In most other countries, the day and month are flipped around. So, typically day, month then year. That's why I didn't realize right away what this column is depicting. It hit me this morning that these are dates. And one date in particular has been needling at me. I think I finally realized why, but I hope I'm wrong."

She clutched her phone.

"Why would you want to be wrong?"

Wouldn't it be a good thing that they were finally making some headway?

She winced then released a miserable-sounding groan. "I was right."

He glanced at the screen again. This time he realized that she was still on the MCPD site looking at a digital version of a missing person poster.

"This girl? Kiana? I know her. I was assigned to be her CASA, but she ran away shortly after we met. I was reassigned to Skylar right after. The date on the poster matches the date that's been tickling my brain."

"Maybe it's a coincidence," Seth suggested, failing to see how that date could possibly be relevant.

Holly paled. Her hand shook as it held the phone, and a sheen of tears glittered in her eyes.

"Seth, look, the date isn't the only number that matches." She pointed at two other numbers on the poster. They lined up with the date listed. "This column here—" she pointed to the number 110 "—matches Kiana's weight. And here—" she tapped on the ledger again, indicating the number 64 "—is her height in inches."

Seth's heart seemed to give a jolt. "That's not a coincidence."

Yet it was hard to fathom.

"Why would someone document Kiana's information like that?"

Holly didn't answer. She scrolled again until she landed on another digital missing person poster.

"Here," she said, her voice shaking, "is another girl. Carola Jameson. Her poster matches this column, though the height would be off by one inch."

She continued to scroll and found another match. Two years in, she finally stopped.

"There are fourteen 'items' listed on the ledger. I've

found three girls that are nearly perfect matches to the data entered."

"Is someone looking for the girls? Keeping track of their information?" Seth wondered.

She walked backward, then slumped, seeming to almost collapse on the edge of the futon.

"Kiana's been on my mind ever since Skylar brought her up yesterday." Holly pinched the bridge of her nose. "Skylar told me Kiana didn't run away. I started thinking about how long she's been gone. The date clicked in my head when I was looking at the ledger. I need to call Mateo."

"I don't understand." Seth's brows furrowed in thought. "I think you're right. The ledger is showing these girls. It's probably likely that the other columns are showing more girls. But why?"

She glanced at him, her dark brown eyes looking huge and haunted.

"This column—" she jabbed at the page once more "—with the biggest number of all..."

"What?" Seth wished he was more of a number person so he could keep up with her.

"I'm afraid this is a dollar amount," she admitted. "I'm afraid this is the amount each girl was sold for."

"I don't understand." Only, the moment the words left his mouth, everything seemed to click into place in his mind.

He felt as if someone had sucker punched him in the heart.

Sold the girls? Now that she explained it, it seemed logical. Unfortunately, despite how horrific it was, it seemed probable.

"I think this is evidence of a human trafficking ring." Holly's voice trembled. "I suspect with his resources,

Mateo will be able to give names to the others on the ledger. I can't help wondering if there are more pages to this ledger. How many children have been sold?"

Seth's heart seemed to thunder in his chest. Could Holly be right? He suspected she was. And while he'd desperately wanted answers, this information was almost too awful to comprehend.

TWELVE

Holly couldn't stop shaking as she spoke with Mateo. She and Seth had moved outside for some privacy. The afternoon sun shone down on them, but the wind had a bitter bite to it, suggesting winter was edging ever closer. She shivered as she hunched inside of her coat.

Holly appreciated Seth's presence beside her.

Solid.

Strong.

Comforting.

She felt almost guilty for it. Who was comforting these girls? There were so many of them. What if there was more than one page to the ledger? Her stomach plummeted at the thought, and her heart twisted in the most agonizing way.

They had to find them.

All of them.

"How sure are you?" Mateo asked when she finished telling him her theory.

"As sure as I can be without having solid proof." Her voice quaked as she tried to remain professional. "Mateo, several of these children are toddlers. Practically babies if I'm reading this information correctly."

Holly didn't miss the way Seth winced.

"I know," Mateo said. "I've been scanning the list as we talked. It's possible some of those listed are boys. They're trafficked as well."

"Of course." Holly's heart ached thinking about it. "I don't understand how ones so little could go missing and they aren't in the news."

"It happens." Mateo's tone was grim. "Sometimes their own parents sell them. Or they slip through the cracks of the foster care system. It's hard to say what happened here."

Holly couldn't help but think of Chloe. She had been in foster care. The thought of her precious daughter slipping through the cracks, of the system failing her, made Holly tremble. She was so grateful for Chloe. Thanked God for her every day.

"You'll be able to look into this right away?"

"I'm making it my top priority." Holly knew Mateo meant it.

He promised to keep her up-to-date on his findings, and they disconnected. Holly slid her phone into her pocket.

Her head was spinning, and she felt nauseated.

She knew that human trafficking had become a problem of epic proportions. She listened to the news. She'd seen the occasional headline. But she'd never given any thought to it happening here. Not in Mulberry Creek.

The idea that Kiana was on the list was almost too much to bear.

"Skylar said that Kiana didn't run away." Her thoughts swirled back to Skylar. "I wonder how much she knows." It suddenly seemed likely that she knew more than she'd let on. "She was clearly scared when we saw her at the courthouse. I knew it was more than just going before the judge."

"Can we get in touch with her?"

Holly tugged out her phone again. She called the teen and was not surprised when it went to voice mail.

"Skylar, call me when you get this, please. It's important." She sent a text as well, knowing the younger generation seemed to prefer that method of communication.

She drummed her fingers on the porch railing. Nervous energy buzzed through her.

"She knows something." Holly was certain of it. "That black car drove by her house before coming here. They must've realized that she's on to something. I wonder if she knows who the woman is and how she's tied to the men who have been trying to kill me." Holly rubbed a hand across her forehead. "I don't understand the link between Teresa, Skylar and the trafficking ring, though. Yet the ledger had to have come from Teresa. Her prints were all over it. It was certainly an older lady I spoke with on the phone. And who drove past Skylar's? Why is Skylar so afraid? Why was the person cruising by also trying to bomb the ranch? I don't understand the connection."

"I don't see what it could be, either. Honestly, I don't want to wait around to find out."

"I was hoping you would say that, Seth. Mateo is working on the rest of the ledger. I want to go check on Skylar. This time, I'm going to make her talk to me. I'll pick her up and carry her to the police station if I must. She needs to tell someone what she knows."

Seth grabbed the keys while Holly checked in on Chloe. Julia and James assured her they didn't mind watching her again.

As soon as they were on their way, Holly tried Skylar once more.

"Still nothing." Holly's tone held equal parts fear and

frustration. "I don't know if I should be worried or if she's simply ignoring me."

"Do you think you should call Alice?"

"We didn't part on the best of terms. I'm afraid she'll tell me not to come."

They were a few blocks down from Alice's house when Holly noticed the cop car parked out front.

Her heart lurched, and a wave of panic washed over her. A cop car in front of someone's house was never a good sign. What had happened? Was Skylar okay? Was Alice? Had the person in the black car gotten to them?

"What's going on here?" Seth said under his breath. He parked the Prius behind the cruiser.

Holly nearly leaped out when it came to a stop. She hustled up the sidewalk and could hear Seth rushing up behind her. She climbed the steps, rang the bell and waited impatiently for what seemed like forever but was probably less than a minute.

Alice opened the door. Her eyes were red and watery. Her face puffy. She held a crumpled tissue and she'd surely been crying.

Holly's heart hammered. "Did something happen to Skylar?"

"Come in." Alice stood back, allowing Holly and Seth entry.

Holly immediately noticed Officer Lainie Hughes standing near the door to the kitchen.

"What happened?" This time, Holly directed her question to the officer because Alice had not responded. "Where's Skylar?"

"It seems that Skylar has run away," Officer Hughes said.

"No," Holly said firmly. "She wouldn't."

Would she? Considering everything that had happened

this week, the unusual way Skylar had been acting, was it possible? Had she been so scared she'd taken off?

Or had someone gotten to her?

Had someone taken her?

The thought hit Holly so hard it nearly made her knees buckle.

Seth placed a hand on her back, offering silent comfort.

"You haven't seen her?" Alice demanded. "I was hoping she'd gone to you."

"We haven't seen her," Seth confirmed when Holly didn't immediately find her voice. "Why do you think she ran away?"

"She left a note," Alice explained. "She said she was tired of this town and everyone in it."

"Are you sure she wrote it?"

"I'm sure, Holly." Alice sniffled. "It's her handwriting. I know she was unhappy after the hearing yesterday. She was upset her father didn't show. But I didn't think she'd leave. The court approved her request and his rights will be terminated."

"She didn't say where she was going?" Holly wrapped her arms around her stomach. She felt ill. "No clue at all?"

Alice tugged a tissue out of her pocket, dabbed at her nose and shook her head.

"Did you notify Jordyn's foster parents?" Holly asked, though in her heart she was sure Skylar wasn't there. Yet she could hope. It would be the best option. "She might feel she needs to see her sister."

"I called them." Alice used a tissue to dab at her eyes. "They haven't seen her but will let me know if she shows up."

"What else are you doing?" Seth asked.

"The department is on the lookout for her locally." Officer Hughes's tone was reassuring.

"Does Detective Bianchi know she's missing?" Holly asked.

"Yes, he's aware of this delicate situation." Officer Hughes's gaze flickered to Alice briefly, and Holly guessed that the officer hadn't shared the information regarding the ledger with Alice. Did she suspect the woman was guilty of something? Or was she simply being discreet until they knew more? "I'm going to head out and go to the bus station. Someone might remember if she was there. I'll keep Detective Bianchi updated."

When the officer had left, Alice turned to Holly. "Do you have any idea where she could have gone?"

"No." Holly shook her head dejectedly.

"We should go." Seth took Holly's hand and gently led her to the door. "Let us know if you find her. We'll do the same and let you know if we hear anything."

They slipped out the door into the chilly air.

"If Skylar isn't here, I don't want to hang around any longer than necessary," Seth said as they hustled down the sidewalk. "I think they tracked us from here once before. I don't want that to happen again."

"I agree. Do you think we could stop to see Shelley? I can't shake the feeling that Skylar is in trouble." Holly winced. "Kids in foster care are going missing. Someone must be covering something up somewhere."

"You think Shelley is a part of that?"

"I sincerely hope not." She raked a hand through her hair. "I'm not ruling anyone out yet, not until Skylar is found. Shelley has been a social worker for a long time. If anyone knows the system, it's her. I want to hear what she has to say about Skylar going missing."

"You want to gauge her reaction."

"I do."

"Do you think Alice is part of it?" Seth's tone was low, as if he hated to even mention it. "Maybe she's pretending Skylar ran away."

"I hope not." Holly blinked back tears. "I just don't know what to think."

As they slid into the Prius, Seth checked the street. Nothing looked out of sorts, yet he, like Holly, couldn't shake the feeling that something was off.

Holly had been tapping away on her phone. She growled in frustration. "I can't find Shelley's address. I don't have any idea where she lives. I wonder if I should bother Mateo with this. He's so busy, but I'm sure he could find her address."

"So could Cassie. Don't forget my sister-in-law is a private investigator. Let me give her a call."

Within minutes they had Shelley's address along with a promise from Cassie that she was praying for Skylar's safe return.

Seth was hypervigilant as he drove. The workday had ended, so there was a fair amount of traffic. It was hard to tell if they were being followed or if there happened to be a lot of people out and about.

"Maybe you should stay in the car," he suggested as he pulled up in front of Shelley's house. "I can talk to her."

"Absolutely not." She sounded adamant. "I'm not sure she'll even talk to me because some of what I want to know about is confidential. I *know* she won't talk if it's you asking the questions."

Seth didn't like it, though he understood. Shelley would likely not want to talk about any of the teens she worked with. He hoped that if they came up with questions that were general enough, she could share some useful information.

They hurried up to the house, and Holly jabbed at the doorbell.

The house seemed still and quiet inside.

Holly rang the bell again.

Seth scanned the street behind them, almost missing the form of a man in the shadows of a house across the street.

"Down!"

He tossed himself at Holly. The two of them hit the porch. Pain seared up his side from the wound he could not seem to stop aggravating. He refused to acknowledge how much it hurt.

The wood around the doorframe splintered where the bullet made contact.

No doubt a silencer was being used.

Seth was grateful for the row of dense bushes that ran along the porch railing. They provided excellent coverage, but would the shooter start shooting into the greenery hoping to get off a good shot?

"Scoot back." He nudged Holly toward the corner of the porch. "Away from where we went down." He drew his Mag and crab-crawled toward the opening of the porch steps. Staying low, making himself as small a target as possible, he aimed his weapon and peered around the railing. A man was creeping their way, but when he saw Seth, he likely noted that Seth was armed and aiming, so he took off running.

Seth was tempted to shoot but didn't want to do so in a residential neighborhood.

When the man disappeared around the corner of the house he'd been creeping along, Seth grabbed Holly and tugged her to her feet.

"He's on the run. Let's get out of here before he comes back."

Or finds backup.

He and Holly raced to the Prius.

Seth did a U-turn, tearing down the street the way they'd come.

They had been shot at again.

Skylar was missing.

And Holly had deciphered a ledger full of missing children.

How had her life gone so sideways?

Now that they were back at the ranch she felt as if she was about to bounce out of her skin. Her nerves were so raw, her worry so intense. Was it possible that Skylar had sent her the ledger? She didn't think so, because she was certainly not the person who had called Holly.

Her mind whirled as she tried to figure out how everything could be connected. She came up with nothing.

"You should eat something. There's plenty of leftovers in the fridge. Mom and Dad will keep Chloe over at Cassie and Eric's for a while longer."

They had texted earlier, letting them know they'd taken Chloe to the other side of the ranch. She was having fun playing with Wyatt. It was for the best because Holly was so distraught, and she didn't want Chloe to see her this way.

"I'm not hungry."

"How about a sandwich?" Seth pressed. "You need to eat something. We don't know how long this could drag on."

No, they didn't know. And that was why Holly was such a ball of nerves. Skylar was out there somewhere.

Holly wanted to do something, anything, to help. But what? They were at a standstill right now.

Please God, show us the way.

"Sure, I'll take a sandwich," Holly said half-heartedly. She didn't say she could eat it.

She followed Seth into the kitchen. The listless feeling that swamped her was almost overwhelming.

"Turkey or ham?"

"Either is fine."

Seth began pulling all the fixings out of the fridge.

Holly pulled a loaf of Julia's homemade wheat bread from the cupboard and then found the plates.

They were halfway through assembling their meal when Holly's phone rang.

She expected it to be Mateo, but her heart seemed to skip a few beats when she saw the name that lit up the screen.

"Skylar?" Holly jabbed at the phone as hope filled her. "I'm with Seth. I want you to know you're on speakerphone."

"It's me." The teen sounded wary.

"We've been so worried about you," Seth said. "We're so glad you called."

"Where are you?" Holly's heart hammered. "Are you all right?"

"Holly, can you come get me? Please?" The teen's voice trembled. "I need you."

"Where are you?" Holly demanded.

"I'm at the Riverside Motel on the edge of town. Do you know where it is?"

"Of course." Holly could picture the seedy dump in her mind. She cringed at the thought of Skylar being in one of the rooms. "It'll take us about twenty minutes to get there."

"I didn't mean to be like Kiana and make you worry." Skylar's voice shook, and it had an odd inflection. "I really didn't."

Holly frowned, confused by the sudden, seemingly out-of-place mention of Kiana. Before she could speak, Skylar rushed on.

"You'll come?"

"Of course." Holly glanced around as she looked for her purse, keys, coat. "What room are you in? I'll leave right now."

Her gaze met Seth's. He raised a questioning brow.

"I'm in one-eleven. No rush." Her tone sounded wobbly. "I'm chilling, eating a cheeseburger."

Holly froze as the seemingly innocuous words sent a frisson of fear down her spine.

"Yeah, you know what I mean," Skylar said, with an odd, strained chuckle. Then her voice changed and became way too somber. "I love you, Holly."

The line disconnected.

"That was—" Seth seemed to search for the word "—strange. She didn't sound quite right."

"No, she didn't." Holly pinched the bridge of her nose, her thoughts whirling. That was one of the oddest phone calls she'd ever had. Nothing about it made sense. "Seth, Skylar is a vegetarian. A strict vegetarian."

"So, it's *really* weird."

"You don't understand." Or maybe it was Holly who misunderstood but she doubted it. "I've asked her if she'll ever eat meat again. She says only under the threat of death. It's kind of become a dumb joke between us. But now is not the time for joking."

Seth's brows hitched. "You don't think—"

"I don't know what to think. But I know Skylar is not eating a cheeseburger right now."

Skylar's words hit her again, this time with stark clarity. *Yeah, you know what I mean.*

"This is bad." Holly pressed a hand over her heart, which continued to race.

"You think she made the phone call under the threat of death."

"Yes. I think that's exactly it."

"She was trying to warn you."

"She also said she didn't mean to be like Kiana. She was adamant that Kiana did not run away. I think Skylar was trying to tell me she didn't run away, either." Holly mentally reviewed every strange word Skylar uttered. "We're pretty sure now that Kiana was taken. I think Skylar was taken as well."

"We need to keep Mateo in the loop."

Holly hesitated because maybe she was jumping to conclusions. "What if I'm wrong?"

"What if you're not?"

Holly hit Mateo's number, and he answered on the second ring.

"I have news," she blurted, then proceeded to tell him about the odd, strained phone call. "Mateo, Skylar said she loved me. She's not the sort of girl who is all warm and fuzzy. Normally, she doesn't show her emotions. She's never said those words to me before. I felt like—" Holly pulled in a breath, not wanting to say the words because she didn't want them to be true "—I felt like she was scared. Like she wasn't sure she would ever see me again so she was saying goodbye."

"You think she was trying to give you clues," Mateo said.

"I'm almost sure of it." Holly's hands trembled. "We need to help her."

"I don't want the two of you going to the motel," he said.

"I can't *not* show up. Skylar's counting on me."

"How do you want to handle this?" Seth asked.

Mateo paused only a beat. "Holly, do you still have that notable bright pink coat with you? The one you had on at the park?"

"Yes."

"And you have access to your Prius?"

"Yes?" The word came out a question because she wasn't sure why that mattered.

"This is what we'll do." He paused again, for only a moment, as if sliding the plan into place in his mind. "I'm calling in Officer Hughes. She's out on patrol looking for Skylar. She'll meet you at the overlook on Wildwood Road right before you get into town. It's about two miles from the motel. She's roughly your size and coloring. She'll take your coat and your car."

"She'll pretend to be me, but then what?"

"You let the department handle the rest," Mateo ordered. "I'll have a full plan in place by the time you meet up with Officer Hughes."

They disconnected.

Holly grabbed her fuchsia coat and her keys, then they raced for her car.

Her whole body buzzed with anxiety as she sent up one prayer after another while they put distance between themselves and the ranch. As Seth drove, she prayed for Skylar to be kept from harm, for safety for Seth and herself. She prayed that Mateo's plan would work and that any law enforcement officers involved would have a hedge of protection around them.

"It's going to be okay." Seth's tone was soothing, confident. "Mateo will put together a solid plan of action. He'll have everything under control in no time."

"You're right." Holly willed herself to believe it. "Skylar is a tough kid. Smart."

"That's for sure."

"I think—"

Holly was interrupted by Seth grumbling something under his breath. She didn't catch what he said, but his tone implied he was rattled.

That was when she heard a series of odd, popping sounds. Then the Prius began to fishtail. Seth grappled with the wheel. A less experienced driver may have lost control, sending the vehicle into a tailspin. He managed to safely pull to the side of the road, but it took some effort because of how fast he'd been driving.

"What happened?" She glanced around the rural, deserted road.

At that moment, a black SUV pulled out from the logging trail ahead. It had been parked off far enough back so as not to be spotted as they drove toward it.

"Tire spikes in the road. They were painted to match the gravel, and I didn't see them in time." Seth's tone was grim. "They were never at the motel. They were luring us away from the ranch. This is a setup. We're in trouble. Big trouble. Call Mateo."

Holly scrambled to pull her phone from her purse. Then her breath caught as the back door of the SUV opened and Skylar stumbled out. Directly behind her, grasping her arm with one hand and holding a gun to her ribs with the other, was Barry Ellis, the escaped prisoner.

Skylar held her head up defiantly. Barry's mouth moved. She shook her head, but he jerked her arm. Scowling, she made a "come here" motion with her hand, clearly signaling that Holly and Seth were to get out of the car.

Holly let out a low moan of terror, not for herself and Seth, but for Skylar.

"I'll stall him. Place that call."

Seth stepped out of the car but left the door open, allowing Holly to hear what was being said. She placed the call. It began to ring.

"Get out of the car!" Barry roared.

The phone was still ringing when the windshield exploded in a spiderweb of shattered glass. A bullet tore into the seat Seth had only moments ago vacated. Skylar screamed. Seth turned, ready to come to her, but Barry shot again. The sound echoed through the air as gravel sprayed far too close to Seth's feet.

Yes, Seth had it right. They were in big trouble.

THIRTEEN

Holly did not dare delay. She placed her phone on the seat, unsure of whether Mateo had answered, if it had gone to voice mail or if it was still ringing. Even as she stepped out of the vehicle, she rattled off their location and the license plate of the SUV.

She prayed that Mateo would, one way or another, hear her.

Barry now had his gun trained on Seth. Though Holly hadn't heard the man's demand, it was evident that he'd ordered Seth to drop his weapon and his phone. Seth did so grudgingly, never taking his eyes off the man who still had a firm grip on Skylar.

"Slide them over," Barry demanded.

Seth did as ordered. He didn't put a lot of effort into it. The gun only slid halfway to Barry. If the man wanted it, he'd have to go get. His phone, which was lighter, flew a bit closer to the criminal.

The driver's-side door of the SUV opened. Holly's breath caught in her throat. For one fuzzy, panicked moment she was grateful that she knew the man behind the wheel. Then in an instant, realization slammed into her, and she realized the familiar face was not there to help.

Judge Cromwell, dressed impeccably in a three-piece

suit, stepped toward her, leveling the gun he held at her chest.

"Miss Nichols," he said coldly, "you have been such a thorn in my side."

Judge Cromwell? It couldn't be.

But it most certainly was.

The missing pieces began to fall into place. They had assumed that Barry Ellis and his cohort had been paid hands. Now it was clear who had been paying them.

"You're the person behind the human trafficking ring?" Holly demanded.

The judge. Someone who was supposed to serve his community.

Judge Cromwell ignored her question. Keeping his gun aimed at her while Barry's remained aimed at Seth, the judge spoke to Holly.

"Where's your phone?"

With one gun pointed at her and the other at Seth, she didn't dare lie.

"In my car."

The judge bobbed his gun toward Skylar. "Fetch it and toss it in the woods. Don't get any silly ideas. This bullet is faster than you are."

Wearing a mutinous expression, Skylar strode toward the Prius. She disappeared into the car for a moment before reappearing. She seemed to hesitate but her face was turned away, and Holly couldn't see her expression.

"Hustle!" Cromwell shouted.

She tossed the phone into the ditch rather than the woods. The judge was too impatient to make her correct the mistake.

"Now get over here," he growled.

She scurried back to them.

"Bind their wrists." He tugged a roll of duct tape from

his jacket pocket. "Be sure to make it tight or we'll have to shoot them both right here, right now. And make it fast!"

He tossed the tape at Skylar. She caught it, and Barry shoved her forward.

"Move!" Barry growled.

Her eyes caught Holly's. They were full of fear and apology.

"It's okay." She didn't want Skylar to do something reckless that would cause trouble for all of them. "Do what he says."

Skylar nodded, but it was clear she was furious about it.

Barry and the judge closed the distance so they were only feet from Seth and Holly, yet they kept their guns trained directly at them.

"Turn around," the judge barked, "so I can see your wrists."

"I'm sorry," Skylar murmured as she began wrapping the tape around Holly's wrists.

"It's not your fault." She tried to keep her tone light for Skylar's sake. The teen wrapped the tape around once, twice, three times until the judge said she could stop. The tape was tight, but Holly had held her wrists apart a bit. She knew it would have some give to it. Probably not enough to matter, but it was something.

Judge Cromwell seemed satisfied and directed Skylar to wrap Seth's in the same way. Once she was finished Barry slid his gun into his waistband and bound Skylar's wrists. Her silver charm bracelet dangled beneath the tape, glittering in the sunlight.

"This is taking too long. We need to move. Now." The judge motioned toward the SUV as he popped the back end open with his key fob. "Get in."

The bound trio were herded to the SUV where they were loaded into the trunk. Barry wrapped their knees and their ankles in tape while the judge ensured their compliance with his pistol. Once they were all loaded in, Judge Cromwell slammed the hatchback. Barry jogged to the middle of the road and swiped up Seth's abandoned weapon. He whipped the phone into the woods.

Holly knew she only had a few precious moments. The three of them were sitting in the rear of the SUV, their backs pressed up against the passenger side. The space wasn't that big, and Seth's legs looked cramped.

"Turn away from me," she commanded Skylar, who was sitting beside her. Holly twisted the opposite way. Her fingers managed to snag around the charm bracelet. She gave a hard tug, despite the limited use of her limbs.

Skylar let out a sharp cry of either pain or protest as the delicate chain broke.

"I'm sorry." Holly turned to face her. "But trust me."

Skylar nodded, and the two men opened the doors and jumped into the front seat.

The whole ordeal on the road had taken less than five minutes. Had Mateo received her call? Was he on the way? How long would it take for him to arrive at this remote area? They would for sure be gone by then. The SUV tore off, leaving a cloud of dust in its wake as they sped away from the crime scene, putting precious miles between them and where Mateo would find any evidence.

She glanced at Seth. He shot her a curious glance, probably wondering why she had pilfered Skylar's bracelet.

Right.

The bracelet. She carefully turned it around in her hands, searching by feel for the charm she needed. There. The heart. It was the only charm with a sharp edge. It took some twisting and maneuvering, but she managed to grip the charm and start making small slashes at the tape that bound her wrists. Her movement was so limited that the act felt almost futile. Yet she couldn't stop. This could be their only chance at freedom.

"How did you end up with these guys?" Seth asked Skylar.

"That man, Barry, came up to me when I was on my way to work. He said I had to go with him. He made me write the note saying I was running away. He had a picture of my little sister Jordyn standing with a group of friends outside her school. He said they would take her as easily as they took me if I didn't do exactly what they said." She gave Holly a miserable look. "I'm sorry. They said I had to lure you out or Jordyn would pay the consequences."

"I understand." Holly knew Skylar would do anything for Jordyn. "You did what you needed to do."

"How does Teresa Krause fit into this?" Holly asked the judge. Her loud voice masked the sound of the tape beginning to break. "Did you kill her?"

Judge Cromwell glanced at them in the rearview mirror.

"No, I didn't kill her." He paused, and his voice was cold with no remnants of the joviality with which he'd greeted Holly in the parking lot of the courthouse. "I didn't kill her because she disappeared, and I haven't been able to find her."

That, at least, was a relief.

"How did she figure you out?" Holly had been mentally reviewing the list of businesses Mateo had given her. "She cleans for your wife's interior design office, doesn't she?" It was one of the nearly two dozen businesses on the list, and until now, Holly had no reason to tie Teresa to the judge and his wife, Breanne.

"You know the saying—no good deed goes unpunished. My wife heard Teresa was having some money troubles, something about being diabetic and having crummy insurance coverage. She asked Teresa if she'd like more hours cleaning since our housekeeper quit when she got married. Teresa mostly does commercial properties, but we asked if she'd be interested in cleaning our house for some extra income. All was going fine until she showed up on the wrong day."

He went on to explain that he'd heard her out in the hallway when he was wrapping up a *business* call. She had pretended she hadn't overheard, but the judge had his suspicions. They kept a close eye on her via their video surveillance at both their home and Breanne's office. They had even bugged Teresa's house. That hadn't turned up anything worrisome. Then, months after the fact, when they thought they were in the clear, they caught Teresa on video picking the lock to Breanne's file cabinet. She'd used her cell phone to take picture after picture of Breanne's records.

"You see," Judge Cromwell continued, "Breanne didn't think it was wise to have this sort of information stored electronically. It is too easy to trace and nearly impossible to erase. Those files, paper copies only, should have been perfectly safe…if not for that meddling woman. Next thing we know, Teresa went home and called you. Thanks to our bugging device, we heard every word." He glared at Holly in the rearview mirror. "*You*, of all people. You're a forensic accountant *and* you're a CASA. And not a CASA for just anyone, but for that little brat who knew too much."

She got what he was saying. Between her career and

her volunteer work, she was a double threat to his scheme. *She* was the common link between Teresa and Skylar. Both of them knew too much, and both of them were connected to Holly now.

"You knew kids were being sold?" Holly asked Skylar.

"I overheard some girls. I wasn't sure. But I suspected. I tried talking to them about it. They told me to forget I heard anything. Someone's been following me, the black car, ever since I moved in with Alice."

"Would that be your wife?" Seth demanded. "Stalking a teenager and trying to bomb my ranch?"

Judge Cromwell chuckled. "What can I say? I married a resourceful woman."

"So you decided to take Holly out of the equation," Seth acknowledged.

Judge Cromwell slid a disgusted look toward Barry, who had failed not once but several times.

"So much for that," the judge scoffed. "Should have hired someone who could get the job done. His brother's as big a failure as he is. I rearranged that brat's court date, bumped it up, just so we knew exactly where you would be and when. I practically handed the two of you to them on a silver platter. What do they do? They mess it up. Lose you in the woods."

Seth and Holly shared a look. If they got out of this, they would be able to tell Mateo who the accomplice was.

"And when he couldn't get the job done and got nabbed," Holly needled, "you had to break him out of jail so he wouldn't snitch."

"Obviously," Cromwell replied.

A few moments later the tape around Holly's wrists made an audible sound as it split from top to bottom. The men up front didn't appear to notice as the SUV's wheels cruised over the gravel road. She bit back a cry of glee. With her hands completely free she was able to move them in front of her. She carefully, quietly, peeled off the remaining tape. Then with one hand she reached behind Seth's back and began to slice away at the tape confining him.

Holly's heart surged with hope. They had a chance to completely free themselves from their bindings. But where were they headed? Would they be able to get free in time? And then what? What awaited them at their destination?

Seth could feel the sharp but dainty edge of the charm gnawing away at the tape. The charm was so small that it was slow going. Too slow. He was itching to have his own bindings gone. He needed to have patience.

"What did you do with Kiana?" Holly demanded as she continued to work. "Where is she?" When the judge remained silent, she went on. "I know you're trafficking children."

"Trafficking, such a ridiculous word," the judge said.

"I don't care what you want to call it." Holly's tone was harsh. "Who did you sell her to?"

Judge Cromwell smirked. "You think you have it all figured out. But you don't."

"Don't I?" Holly snarked back.

The judge stayed silent, gloating.

Seth felt some give in the tape. As soon as a weak spot was created, the rest of the tape gave away quickly.

He knew he needed to keep the conversation going, so their captors remained distracted. Also, there were questions that they wanted answers for.

"We know you're selling these children." He moved slowly, discreetly, shifting subtly as he brought his hands to the front of his body. He was grateful the back seat of the vehicle blocked the judge's view of them from essentially the neck down. "The ledger proves it."

"The ledger?" Judge Cromwell's voice was nearly a growl. "What ledger?"

Seth didn't miss the furious glare the judge shot his accomplice.

"The ledger Teresa Krause sent to me," Holly said. "You know, the one that documents the sale of children."

Judge Cromwell backhanded Barry. "You told me you confiscated the files sent by that woman."

"I did!" Barry shot back. "You know I did. You said yourself I did good intercepting the file that showed how you and your missus were laundering money through her interior design business."

"That lady must've sent more than one file," Cromwell realized.

That made sense. The file that had reached Holly had seemed minimal. If another, more substantial file had been sent earlier, one that hadn't reached her, it would explain how Teresa thought the information could be helpful.

"You're not going to get away with this." Holly sounded confident. "Detective Bianchi has a copy of the ledger. He knows Mrs. Krause is involved and has her client list. If we go missing, he'll piece everything together before you know it."

The judge stayed silent.

"Is Shelley in on this?" Holly asked, mentioning Skylar's caseworker.

Holly had pulled her legs up and was now slicing away at the bindings around her knees. Seth wanted to take the charm from her, slice his own bindings free, but he fought for patience again.

"No, the kids on her caseload are too old. I have plenty

of other caseworkers who see things the way I do and who are happy to help me out."

"How do you see things?" Seth demanded.

"You think you have it figured out, but you don't. They aren't being trafficked. These kids you are so concerned about are going to homes with parents who love them."

Seth and Holly shared a confused look.

Now completely free, Holly handed the heart charm to him.

Skylar shifted, obviously anxious for her turn. He couldn't blame the girl, but he needed to be the first line of defense when they reached their destination.

He took the charm and started on the tape binding his legs. He didn't know where they were headed or how much longer they would be in this vehicle. It was crucial he was prepared to fight. He discreetly cut away at the tape as the judge talked.

"The kids are going to parents who are willing to pay top dollar for them. For whatever reason, the adoption system has failed them, or maybe they want to hurry the process along, so they come to me. It's a win-win. These kids are in the foster system for a reason. I take them out of crummy situations. I put them with families who are willing to spend big money to get them. The kids grow up in decent homes. The parents have the child they always wanted, and my wife and I get a little richer with each transaction."

That made no sense.

"Kiana and Carola are not small children." Holly frowned. "They wouldn't acclimate well to a new family. So—"

"Both pregnant." The judge cut her off. "We could not care less about the two of them, but their newborn infants are *very* appealing to us."

A gasp of horror escaped her lips.

Seth understood her alarm. The missing girls were pregnant. And he planned to take their babies from them and sell them, likely without their consent. It was repugnant.

"They got themselves into a little bit of trouble," Cromwell said. "Same as a whole list of girls before them. I'd say you have no idea what a newborn goes for on the black market, but considering you saw the ledger I'd say you do know. We got a nice down payment upon procurement—"

"Upon kidnapping the mothers," Holly growled.

"—and we'll get another nice chunk upon delivery."

Delivery of the newborns.

"Did you do your due diligence with these parents? Vet them at all?" Seth was seething. "Do you know for a fact these kids are going to loving homes? People who are willing to buy children don't strike me as upstanding citizens." Seth cringed, thinking of the horrors these children could potentially face.

The judge made a noncommittal sound, as if that was not his problem.

"The toddlers on the ledger... They were adopted?" Holly asked.

"Sure were." Cromwell tapped his hand against the steering wheel. "Most couples want babies, but some will settle for a cute little thing if they're young enough to have their memories fade away. Your little girl sure is a pretty child. A little older than we're usually interested in, but lovely enough she would've brought in a nice chunk of change from the right client."

Cromwell glared at Barry again, clearly angry that the hired hand had blundered the job.

Barry mumbled something unintelligible.

Seth got the last of his bindings free. He surreptitiously passed the charm bracelet back to Holly so she could work on Skylar's wrists.

Thank You, Lord. Please continue to protect us.

"You were going to kill me." Holly's voice was strained. "And then sell my daughter?"

"That was the plan," Cromwell agreed.

Holly made a guttural sound in her throat.

Anger coursed through Seth. They were not going to let this evil man win. Bringing sweet, innocent Chloe into this mess ratcheted Seth's determination to a whole new level.

Holly discreetly leaned to the side. Seth knew she had set to work on Skylar's bindings. He had to wonder how much longer they were going to be on the road. Both of their captors had guns. He had only his military training. It would have to be enough, because at the moment he was weaponless.

"Where are you taking us?" he demanded.

"I see no point in being secretive," Cromwell admitted. "You'll find out anyway. Breanne's granddad willed her his run-down ranch. There haven't been animals here for years. We lease the land to the nearest neighbor for his corn crop. The house serves another purpose."

Seth cringed. He could only imagine the sort of things Cromwell would use a place like that for.

The vehicle took a sharp left. Seth glanced around. They were the only vehicle out on this back road. Hope that Mateo would find them was dwindling. Too many miles were between them and the crime scene.

"What does Breanne think of you tarnishing her family heritage this way?"

Cromwell chuckled. "Well, Holly, whose idea do you think it was to use the place?"

Seth scowled, disgusted by it all. Then his heart rate kicked up a notch. The vehicle was slowing. Skylar's wrists were free. Holly had handed off the charm. Now the teen was using the sharp edge of the heart to work on the tape around her knees.

It was a good thing, too, because he was sure they were getting close to their destination. The SUV turned onto a gravel drive that led to a decrepit house. The white paint had seen better days decades ago. It was chipped, peeling, and the red front door seemed like an incongruous afterthought. The property was surrounded by a field stubbled with harvested corn on one side, a thin forest on the other. The crop would've been harvested at least a month ago, giving no reason for anyone to come this way.

They had been driving for quite some time. Seth was familiar with the area, but with all the unnecessary turns and the back road driving, he wasn't sure as to their exact whereabouts. He couldn't imagine that Mateo would ever be able to track them here.

It didn't matter, he decided. He was a trained combat veteran. Now that his hands and legs were free, he would do whatever needed to be done.

"Let's get this taken care of," Cromwell said to Barry. "This time, there's no room for error. Stick to the plan and don't mess things up."

"Yes, sir." Barry's tone was less than respectful. He glanced back at them and grinned. "The ranch is hundreds of acres. Lots of room to bury bodies."

Chuckling, he got out of the vehicle.

Seth pulled in a calming breath. These men were not going to get the best of them.

Skylar whimpered as Holly harshly muttered, "We'll see about that."

She patted her coat pocket and Seth noticed a bulge

but didn't have time to contemplate what she was checking for.

"Stay behind me." He hurriedly repositioned himself. The dark windows worked in his favor as Cromwell and Barry couldn't see his movement. When the hatchback popped up, Seth's legs shot out, hitting each man square in the chest.

The judge flew backward, landing on his rump as his gun went flying. Barry staggered but maintained his balance. Seth didn't give him the chance to get his bearings. He leaped out of the SUV and plowed into him, punching him in the gut and taking him down. They struggled over the gun. Barry tried swinging at Seth's abdomen, clearly remembering the wound he'd inflicted. He got in a good punch that filled Seth's brain with blinding pain.

Seth was vaguely aware of the judge clambering to his feet. Then he screamed as Holly blasted him with the bear spray Cassie had armed her with days ago.

So that's what she'd had in her pocket.

Cromwell fell to his knees, and guttural groans spilled from his mouth as he rubbed at his eyes.

Barry had a death grip on his weapon. Just when the assaulted gash in Seth's side was so excruciating he didn't think he'd be able to fight the man a moment longer, Holly darted toward them, pulled the cover off a travel mug and dumped steaming coffee on the man's face. He screamed, released the pistol and sputtered as he scrubbed the blinding liquid from his eyes.

Seth grabbed the gun and rolled away, grunting in pain. He'd busted his stitches open. Every last one of them, if he wasn't mistaken. He could feel blood trickling down his side. He'd have to deal with that later.

He grabbed the gun and pointed it at Barry. "Stay

where you are." He glanced at the judge and was satisfied he was still incapacitated.

"I found this." Skylar held the roll of duct tape that had been used to bind them earlier. "Can we use it?"

"Absolutely," Holly said.

"Hands in front of you," Seth ordered Barry. "I am completely out of patience. Don't tempt me to shoot."

Heeding Seth's warning, the man lowered his hands. Skylar handed Holly a long strip of the tape. Holly wrapped the man's wrists, round and round. Then wrapped his knees, just to be on the safe side. Next, they restrained the judge in the same way. For good measure, she slapped a piece of tape over each of their mouths.

They had found out all they needed to know for now. They would let Mateo figure out the rest.

"That was quick thinking," Holly told Skylar, "grabbing the coffee like that."

"I spotted it when I was looking for the tape."

Holly frowned. "Seth, you're hurt, again."

"Nah, it's nothing."

Skylar gave him a skeptical look. "That doesn't look like nothing."

He didn't have a chance to argue. Banging from above caught their attention. They all whirled to face the second story of the run-down house.

A dark-haired girl stood in a window, pounding on the glass.

Holly gasped.

"That's Kiana," Skylar said. A moment later a smaller redhead stepped beside her. "And that's Carola."

Both girls now thumped on the window. Seth could hear their shouts for help.

Gripping his Mag, he strode toward the house, knowing their ordeal wasn't over yet.

FOURTEEN

Holly darted after Seth, and they raced up the rickety steps. She wished she had her phone. It would have been reassuring to call Mateo for backup. That wasn't an option. They would get the girls, load the two criminals in the driveway into SUV and take them to the police station.

Seth gripped the doorknob and gave it a turn. The door opened easily.

"Stay behind me." Gun drawn, he cautiously stepped over the threshold.

Holly let out a gasp of horror as a woman lunged at him from behind the door. He twisted sideways as she swung an iron skillet at him. It connected with the back of his head rather than his face.

Furious and tired of being the victim, Holly lunged at the woman whom she recognized as Judge Cromwell's wife. She was not going to allow Breanne to strike Seth again. The two went down, and the skillet went flying. Then Seth was there, obviously in pain, but still taking command of the situation. He gripped the woman's flailing hands.

"Skylar, the duct tape," he ordered.

Holly glanced over her shoulder as Skylar turned to

dart out the door. The teen stopped, let out a shriek of surprise and came stumbling back inside as a large man stepped in, filling the doorframe.

Holly's body seemed to droop in relief. "It's okay, Skylar. It's Detective Bianchi."

"Looks like I'm a little too late." The detective strode in, gun drawn as he scanned the area to be sure there were no more threats. Officer Hughes came in behind him.

"Cuff her," he told the officer as he nodded toward Breanne.

In moments, Breanne was detained, just as her husband and Barry Ellis were.

"There are two girls upstairs. Two of the missing girls."

Holly stepped back, allowing the officers who accompanied Mateo to do their jobs. Officer Hughes dashed up the stairs along with a male officer Holly didn't recognize.

"Are we ever glad to see you." Seth winced as he spoke to Mateo. "How did you find us?"

Mateo glanced at Holly. "My voice mail picked up in the middle of your attack on the road. Holly rattled off the license plate number of the SUV. Then I assume this one—" he nodded toward Skylar "—got on the line briefly and said you all were being kidnapped by Allen Cromwell. Things got muffled after that."

Holly recalled the girl's hesitation on the road, the way her face had been turned away from them all briefly before she tossed the phone into the ditch.

"I saw a call had been placed," Skylar explained. "I didn't know who was on the line, but I knew someone would be looking for you."

Holly pulled the girl into a quick hug.

"We checked their home, Mrs. Cromwell's business downtown, and when we came up empty both places, we ran a property records check and found this place under their name. We got here as soon as we could."

Sirens blared in the distance.

"That'll be the backup I called for." Mateo arched a brow at Seth. "Looks like you could use some medical assistance."

"I'm fine." Seth scowled as he touched the ridiculously large lump on his head. "This ordeal is finally over, and that's got me feeling pretty good."

He glanced at Holly. Her heart swelled with relief... and...love?

When he held his arms out to her, she stepped into them.

"It's over," he murmured into her hair. "You're safe."

Holly believed him with every ounce of her being.

Seth wasn't sure what was more frustrating: having to stay overnight in the hospital for observation of his freshly stitched knife wound and concussion, or having his little sister hovering over him. The blurry vision he'd suffered after the attack yesterday hadn't been real appealing, either. It had landed him in the hospital for observation. Fortunately, this morning that particular affliction had abated.

"It wasn't good enough that you got yourself stabbed—" Nina scanned over his chart, even though she was not on duty and not even his nurse "—but you had to go and get yourself concussed, too. Not cool, big bro. Not cool at all."

She was teasing, he knew, but it was annoying all the same.

"I'll be more careful next time," he grumbled.

"See that you are." She winked at him.

He rolled his eyes.

"Can I go home yet?"

"Soon." She put his chart back on the hook on the end of the bed. "I've called dibs on pushing you out in your wheelchair."

If she was standing closer, he would've smacked her with his pillow. Patients weren't really pushed out in wheelchairs. That only happened in movies. Right? All he knew was that he would be walking out on his own two feet.

A knock at the door pulled Nina's attention away from him. She glanced at the clock with a frown. Though she wasn't on duty, she *was* using her employee privileges to be here this early. Seth knew she was making sure visiting hours had started. Satisfied that she wasn't breaking any rules, she opened the door.

Seth was glad he wasn't required to be hooked to a heart monitor because he was sure his skipped several beats when he realized it was Holly coming to visit. Once he'd been whisked away to the hospital yesterday, he hadn't had a chance to see her again. He had been doctored up and questioned.

Holly had been questioned as well. Then she'd gone back to the ranch to be with Chloe. He'd been disappointed she hadn't come to see him, but he understood Chloe needed her.

Though it hadn't even been a full day, he had missed her and was grateful she was here now.

Skylar walked in behind Holly, carrying a gift basket of some sort.

Nina greeted the pair, then excused herself, allowing them some privacy.

"You don't seem like the daisy type," Skyler smirked, "so I got you something else you might enjoy."

Seth looked at the basket and grinned. Sitting inside the large popcorn bowl was a bag of organic popcorn, a variety of seasonings, several boxes of chocolate-covered raisins and a two-liter bottle of soda.

"I figured you're going to have to take it easy for a while. You might as well watch a movie or two," Skylar explained.

"This is great." He reached over and gave her hand a friendly squeeze. "You were brave, and I'm really proud of you. That was quick thinking with the coffee and the duct tape. Not to mention telling Mateo who had us."

"Thanks." Her eyes darted around the room, and she toyed with the bracelet that had helped save them all. The links had easily been squeezed back together so she hadn't been without it for long. "I wish I'd come forward sooner, but I was afraid of telling anyone what I knew."

Seth's gaze flashed to Holly. She wore a look of sympathy and obviously already knew what was troubling Skylar.

"What did you know?"

Skylar glanced at Holly, as if looking for permission. Or perhaps encouragement. Holly gave her a subtle nod.

Skylar turned back to Seth.

"I lived in a group home before I lived with Alice. I heard rumors from some of the other girls that kids were disappearing. Worse, I heard that they were being sold with the help of caseworkers. At first, I didn't believe it. You know, some people like to gossip and cause trouble and spread lies to stir things up." She paused, as if she needed a moment to mentally regroup. "Then Kiana disappeared, and I knew something was wrong.

We weren't exactly friends, but we were in the same group home. I knew she liked school and that she was smart. She couldn't wait to graduate. A month before she went missing, she'd been accepted into a technical college with plans to become a dental hygienist. It made no sense that she would run away. I mentioned that to a few of the girls, but I was afraid to say anything to Shelley or the house mother because I had no way of knowing if they were in on it. Next thing I knew, I was being sent to live with Alice. I think one of the girls ratted me out to someone. Then that black car started following me around. I started receiving pictures in the mail of my sister at school. I knew I had to keep my mouth shut. I was scared to death. Not for me, but for Jordyn."

"That's just not right." Seth truly felt for the teen who had been through so much at such a young age. "No one should make you feel that way."

Holly put a hand on Skylar's shoulder. The girl gave her a brief smile, then continued her story.

"When you and Holly showed up and the car drove by, I panicked. Alice was really nice when I first moved in. Then she started acting strange. Shelley, too, and she'd been my caseworker for years. I was scared, didn't know who I could trust."

Seth imagined it was hard enough for a foster child, someone who had no one to rely on, to trust someone under the best of circumstances, which these were not.

He shot a look at Holly as his heart sank. He remembered how they'd huddled together at the courthouse, how they'd shut down their conversation when Holly had neared. "Are Alice and Shelley a part of this?"

"No," Skylar said quickly. "They were being secretive but for an entirely different reason."

She went on to explain that Alice hoped to adopt her but that she was nervous because she didn't know if the judge would agree to terminate Skylar's father's parental rights. Or if Skylar would even want her to. As it turned out, now that Skylar knew the truth, she very much wanted to be adopted.

"That's great. I'm really happy for you."

"The best part is she's been talking to the family who is adopting Jordyn. They agreed we should get to spend time together." Skylar's eyes glittered with happy tears. "That's something else she was keeping secret. She didn't want to get my hopes up until she knew they would agree. But they did."

Seth was sure he could actually feel the happiness radiating off this girl.

"That's fantastic." Despite how they sometimes squabbled, he couldn't imagine being kept from his siblings. "I hope everything falls into place quickly for you."

"Thanks." Skylar glanced at the door, then back at Seth. "It was really nice seeing you, but Alice is waiting for me in the lobby."

He flashed her a smile. "I'm glad you stopped by. I hope I see you around."

"Maybe you can join me and Holly sometime for a veggie burger."

Seth chuckled. "Sure. Sounds like a plan."

After Skylar left, Seth looked at Holly. "That's so great to hear that she's getting a happy ending."

"Actually, I think it's more like a happy beginning," Holly corrected. "I'm still her CASA for the time being. I had breakfast with her and Alice bright and early this morning. I have a good feeling about the adoption. Though I'm not happy she didn't tell me about her plans, she wasn't obligated to. I understand she was nervous to mention it until she knew she could move forward. As a CASA my allegiance is to the foster child, not the foster parent."

"Makes sense."

"There's more good news," Holly continued. "Mateo called to let me know that Teresa Krause came forward."

His eyebrows hitched. "I take it she's alive and well then."

Holly went on to explain that Teresa had overheard the judge talking about selling a baby. She waited so long to come forward because she was sure she had misheard or that he had been joking. She couldn't believe such a well-respected man could be part of something so vile. Yet as the weeks went by, she couldn't stop thinking about it. She didn't dare make an accusation without proof.

"So she got her proof." Seth nodded as the pieces of the story all started to make sense.

"Then everything went sideways. When she heard I was attacked, she knew they were on to her and went on the run. She was able to give Mateo a copy of the complete file that she sent, the one that was intercepted by Barry. She claims it shows how the payments were laundered through Breanne's business." Holly blew out a breath. "I'll be looking over that information real soon. Originally, she wasn't going to send the ledger, because the information was so vague and she didn't think it was relevant. It was sent as an afterthought in case it could help. We're fortunate that she sent that second file. It wasn't much—"

"But it was enough." Enough for Holly's brilliant mind to figure things out. "Where has she been?"

"Apparently she and her late husband were avid outdoors people. She decided to go off-grid. She's been staying at a free backwoods campsite a few hours from here. Somewhere that she didn't have to show ID. She had a battery-operated radio with her that she kept tuned into a local station for news. Once she heard the Cromwells were apprehended she knew it was safe to come back."

"Has Kevin Ellis been caught?"

"Yes, they caught Barry's brother late last night. Once Mateo knew who they were looking for, it didn't take long to track him down."

"The girls? Kiana and Carola?"

"They'll receive counseling and already have a safe place to stay. Kiana is determined to keep her baby. Carola is due soon and knew from the start she wants an open adoption for her child."

A sharp knock sounded on the door. Dr. Rosetti didn't wait for a response before stepping inside.

"I heard you're anxious to get out of here," she said.

Seth flashed the doctor a grin. "You heard right."

He was happy to see the doctor who had treated him yesterday, but disappointed that Holly stepped toward the door.

"Cassie was kind enough to take Chloe this morning. I need to go get her. I'm glad you're going home soon. I should get out of the way." She turned to leave.

"Holly, wait!"

She pivoted back around.

There was so much he wanted to say. A hospital room, especially with a doctor hovering nearby, was not the place. Yet if he didn't say something soon, he'd lose his nerve.

"Could you maybe come over to the ranch tonight?"

She hesitated.

"Please." He could hear the raw emotion in his voice and suspected she had to hear it, too. He couldn't let her walk out this door, out of his life. Not again. Not after everything they'd been through. He decided he had nothing to lose. "If you walk out this door and I don't see you again, I'm going to miss you something fierce."

She looked momentarily stunned, then a beautiful smile lit her face. "I'll bring us dinner."

He grinned, relieved by her response as he felt a spark of hope for the future. "I can't wait."

It had taken a great deal of effort on Seth's part to clear everyone out of his house before Holly's expected arrival. Nina had been hovering, his parents had been questioning, and even Cassie and Eric had stopped by to see if there was anything they could help with.

He'd said yes, they could help by having the family over for dinner so he could have some time alone with Holly.

Now here he was, pacing in his own hallway, too nervous to try to sit and relax. His thoughts were so entrenched in Holly, Chloe and his hope for the future that he barely noticed his injuries at all.

When her Prius came down the driveway his heart took off at a gallop. He was grateful Eric had taken care of repairs.

Seth trained his gaze heavenward.

"I could really use Your help, Lord. I love this lady, and I might only have one chance at letting her know. Please, give me the words I need to touch her heart."

He knew now, without a doubt, that he loved her and did not want to live without her.

Their adventure in the wilderness, the night spent

lost in the deer stand, was enough outdoor adventure to last him for a lifetime. He didn't need white water rafting, mountain biking or hiking through rugged terrain. He wanted something else. Stability, family and a home filled with love were what he craved.

He opened the door before Holly had a chance to knock.

Her hair was pulled back in its usual tight, high, tidy ponytail. Her cheeks were rosy, and her eyes had a sparkle he hadn't seen in years.

"Where's Chloe?"

"She's with Melanie. Melanie asked if she could babysit again, but her parents and I agreed it would be best for her to do it at their house, with her parents right there, for now."

"Good idea," Seth said, though he would've like to have seen Chloe.

"I brought beef stew." She gripped a soup tureen. One arm was looped through the handle of a wicker basket. "And cheddar biscuits. Homemade brownies for dessert." She wrinkled her nose adorably. "You always used to say brownies were your favorite."

"They still are." He took the tureen and basket from her so she could remove her coat and hang it up. Then he led her to the kitchen where he placed everything on the table. He turned to her. "This smells fantastic, and I can't wait to eat, but I think we need to talk first."

She bit her lip and nodded.

Where did he begin?

"Holly, the moment I saw you on that road and realized it was *you*, it was like I was transported back in time. Everything I felt for you came rushing back." He took her hands. "I loved you back then. What this past week has taught me is that I love you still. When you kissed me in the deer stand, I hoped it meant you felt that way, too. That you were looking for a new start. Closure is not what I want from you."

She gave him a tremulous smile. "I don't want closure, either. I also don't want to keep you from your dreams. But the thought of you leaving my life again is almost too much to bear. We could try the long-distance thing. Or I could move if it's not too soon for me to follow you to Bozeman when you go. Georgina would probably let me work remotely. Or I could get a new job. I've even thought about going off on my own and opening my own business. I could—"

"Hush." Seth pressed a finger to her lips. "You're not moving anywhere."

"Okay," she whispered when his hand fell away. Her smile slid from her face. "I'm sorry. I got carried away. It was silly of me to think you'd want me—"

"Holly, I *do* want you. What I'm trying to say is that you're not moving anywhere. And neither am I. I want to stay here to build a life with you and Chloe and whatever other children God blesses us with. Biological, adopted. I don't care. I want a family. With you."

She stared at him for a moment but didn't say anything.

"Holly?" He squeezed her hand. "What's going through your head?"

"I'm trying to wrap my mind around the realization we've come full circle. God in His infinite wisdom knew I needed time. Time to grow. Time to find myself, learn to love myself and appreciate my own worth. I couldn't believe you truly loved me back then because I felt so… unlovable. But finding the Lord changed me."

"I needed time, too," Seth admitted. "I needed the

military. I needed to learn responsibility. I took my life, my family, all my liberties for granted."

"Where do we go from here?"

Dating, at this point, after everything they had been through seemed so trivial. He knew this woman. Had known her and loved her for years.

Letting go of her hand, he lowered himself to one knee.

Her eyes widened, and she gasped.

Seth gave her a questioning look. A silent invitation to tell him to stop right here, right now, if she didn't want what she had to know was coming.

He pulled a small burgundy box from his pocket.

"Holly, I bought this ring for you a decade ago." He paused while she pressed a hand to her mouth and blinked back tears. "Something has told me to hold on to it for all these years. It might not be the biggest, fanciest ring, but I bought it with love. I loved you then. I love you still."

Her breath hitched.

"Will you marry me?"

"Yes!"

She grabbed his arm and insistently tugged him back to his feet. Mindful of the stitches in his side, she hugged him tight. When she let go, he slipped the ring onto her finger. The band was lovely and ornate, but the emerald-cut diamond was small.

"I could afford something bigger, better now—"

"No." She shook her head as she held her hand out, gazing at her ring. "I love it. It's perfect. You really bought this for me? All those years ago?"

He nodded.

"I had no idea." She swiped at the moisture on her cheeks. "You bought me a ring…and I left you with nothing but a letter."

"Hey, it's okay."

"I'm so sorry," she whispered. "We could have had so much time together."

"Don't be sad for the time we lost. Be grateful for the experiences we gained. I love you and appreciate you more than ever before. You found a faith in God you didn't have, raised a beautiful daughter, have helped foster kids who would've been lost without you. You've done great things, Holly." He laughed. "It's not like we're ancient. God willing, we have a long, beautiful life ahead of us."

"You always did know what to say."

"I speak the truth. I want you. I want Chloe. I want us to have a life together. *You* are what's been missing from my life. The both of you. It took finding you again to realize that."

"I don't want to waste any more time."

"Then let's get married tomorrow."

She laughed.

He didn't.

Her eyes widened. "You're not serious."

"Sure am. I loved you a decade ago. I loved your heart. I loved your brilliance. I loved you with every cell in my body. Still do, and nothing is going to change that. So why wait?" He paused, his expression darkening. "Unless you don't feel the same."

"Of course I feel the same!" She beamed at him. "And I cannot think of anything else I want more in this world than to marry you as soon as possible."

"Maybe tomorrow is a little soon," he murmured. "But you are going to Mrs. Montgomery before the month is through."

"I'm counting on it."

When she kissed him, he knew he'd found his other

half. It was as if his heart had found the missing piece
and was now whole.

He gave all the glory to God for finally, at long last,
bringing the two of them together despite the mistakes
they had made that had kept them apart. He knew in his
heart it was the Lord's plan that had reunited him with
the love of his life.

EPILOGUE

It had been months since Holly had last been in this courtroom. Judge Allen Cromwell would never preside in this space again. All of the children who had been sold were now recovered, and their new caseworkers were diligently trying to place them in homes that would love them.

Judge Athena Radzinski was seated at the bench today. She smiled at the group streaming in.

The entire Montgomery family was here for the proceeding. Even Aunt Viv had come today to support Holly and Chloe.

Skylar was here with Alice. Her adoption would also be finalized soon, and then Holly would no longer be her CASA. Holly would eventually find another young girl to support. It was her calling, and one she would not ignore.

Everyone took a seat in the rows of long benches lining the back half of the room. They had always reminded Holly of church pews. Today, like the day she adopted Chloe, she was directed toward the table at the front of the room. Seth moved beside her, holding Chloe's hand.

Once they were seated, Judge Radzinski asked Chloe, "Do you know why you're here today?"

Chloe's head bobbed. Her curls bounced, and her eyes sparkled.

"I'm getting a daddy." Her excitement was so evident that everyone chuckled. "He's the *best*."

Holly and Seth had married less than two weeks after he had proposed. They had pulled the wedding together as quickly as possible as neither had wanted to wait a day longer than necessary.

The last few months couldn't have been any more blissful. Holly and Chloe already loved life on the ranch. Holly loved married life. She loved having a big, loud, extended family. In fact, her life was so filled with love these days she felt as if her blessings were constantly overflowing.

Seth had made it clear he wanted to become Chloe's father. Today was the first open day on the judge's docket.

So here they were.

As the court proceeding progressed, Holly's heart was so full she felt it may burst. When it was over, they walked out of the courthouse as a family, hand in hand.

"Guess what," Wyatt said to Chloe as they walked down the steps. "Now you're my cousin."

"I know," Chloe said seriously. "My mommy told me you would be. I've never had a cousin before. I have a grandpa and grandma now, too."

Wyatt nodded solemnly. "I have to share mine with you. But that's okay."

Holly glanced over her shoulder to check on Vivienne. Nina had her by the elbow and was guiding her down the steps. The young nurse and the elderly woman had hit it off when Nina had chauffeured her to Mulberry Creek this morning. Now they were in giggly conversation.

"You know," Seth said as he leaned close and whispered in her ear, "the proceeding today got me thinking. Chloe would be a great big sister."

Holly felt her heart rate kick up a notch. She grinned. "I'm glad you think so."

"What I think is that we should explore adoption. Work on getting her a baby brother. Or sister."

Holly stopped at the bottom of the steps and faced him. She tapped a finger against her chin and pretended to be lost in thought. "Or…we could *have* a baby this time around."

"I suppose we could," he said as if he was just playing along.

She grabbed his hand and squeezed. "We *are*."

"We are?" He blinked at her in surprise. It took several long moments for him to wrap his head around what she was saying. "Wait. For real?"

She nodded, barely able to contain her joy. "I found out this morning. It's been so hectic I haven't had a chance to tell you. I was going to wait until we were home and had a bit of privacy, but since you brought it up…"

He whooped for joy. Then he picked her off her feet and swung her around before placing her back on the ground and pressing a loud, ecstatic kiss to her forehead. He didn't seem to care that everyone was giving them questioning looks.

Seth grinned. "I'm just so glad to be a dad."

"I'd say so." Eric chuckled. "It is pretty great."

Happy with that answer, the group continued toward the parking lot.

Seth gripped Holly's hand.

"Having you back in my life is the answer to my most heartfelt prayer."

"Mine, too. God is good."

Oh yes, she thought as she silently counted her abundant blessings, *God is so very good.*

* * * * *

If you liked this story from Amity Steffen,
check out her previous
Love Inspired Suspense books,

Reunion on the Run
Colorado Ambush
Big Sky Secrets

Available now from Love Inspired Suspense!
Find more great reads at www.LoveInspired.com.

Dear Reader,

I am sincerely grateful that you chose to follow Seth and Holly on their journey. So many people, like young Holly, question their worth. It was only when she discovered the unfathomable depth of the love bestowed upon her by her Lord and Savior that she realized how much her life mattered. *She* mattered, as does each and every one of us.

God loves us so much that He gave us His only Son. Through Him, though we are broken we are healed, and though we are sinners we are forgiven. We are worthy, loved and redeemed.

Holly had to learn to love herself before she was able to accept how much Seth loved her.

I hope you'll continue following the Montgomery siblings. I'm currently working on Nina and Mateo's story. I'm so excited to share it with all of you.

Blessings,
Amity

COMING NEXT MONTH FROM
Love Inspired Suspense

BABY PROTECTION MISSION
Mountain Country K-9 Unit • by Laura Scott
When his sister is abducted, rancher Cade McNeal will do anything to keep his newborn nephew safe from a kidnapper's clutches. But as danger escalates, he'll need Officer Ashley Hanson and her K-9 partner to help evade the assailants on their tail and find his sister...*before* time runs out.

TRACKING THE TRUTH
Security Hounds Investigations • by Dana Mentink
After Emery Duncan is kidnapped and dumped in a lake, Roman Wolfe and his bloodhound rescue her from an icy death. Someone doesn't want her to find out what really happened the night her father confessed to attempted murder. Can Roman protect Emery and her baby nephew long enough to discover the truth?

COLD CASE TARGET
Texas Crime Scene Cleaners • by Jessica R. Patch
Sissy Spencer finds herself in a killer's crosshairs after she walks in on a man trying to murder her friend. When her ex-boyfriend, private investigator Beau Brighton, saves her, she knows she must rely on him to stay alive. Only protecting Sissy becomes a dangerous game when they unravel her terrifying connection to a serial killer...

ROCKY MOUNTAIN SURVIVAL
by Jane M. Choate
Someone's willing to kill for photojournalist Kylie Robertson's photos. After she's attacked, she flees to the only person she trusts—her ex, former navy SEAL Josh Harvath. Can they piece together the mystery behind the images *and* their past...or will they fall victim to unknown enemies?

TREACHEROUS ESCAPE
by Kellie VanHorn
Biochemist Vienna Clayton makes a groundbreaking discovery—and now she's framed for her boss's murder, her laptop is stolen and gunmen are after her. She escapes, but park ranger Hudson Lawrence saves her when her boat is capsized. Together, they must clear her name and uncover the true culprits...before she's silenced for good.

COLORADO DOUBLE CROSS
by Jennifer Pierce
Determined to prove his partner's death was a setup, DEA agent Nick Anderson goes undercover in a drug cartel. Only now he and his partner's widow, Alexis White, are caught up in a lethal web of deception, corruption and murder...and they could be the next to die.

LOOK FOR THESE AND OTHER LOVE INSPIRED BOOKS WHEREVER BOOKS ARE SOLD, INCLUDING MOST BOOKSTORES, SUPERMARKETS, DISCOUNT STORES AND DRUGSTORES.

LISCNM0224

Get 3 FREE REWARDS!

We'll send you 2 FREE Books plus a FREE Mystery Gift.

FREE
Value Over
$20

Both the **Love Inspired®** and **Love Inspired®** Suspense series feature compelling novels filled with inspirational romance, faith, forgiveness and hope.

YES! Please send me 2 FREE novels from the Love Inspired or Love Inspired Suspense series and my FREE gift (gift is worth about $10 retail). After receiving them, if I don't wish to receive any more books, I can return the shipping statement marked "cancel." If I don't cancel, I will receive 6 brand-new Love Inspired Larger-Print books or Love Inspired Suspense Larger-Print books every month and be billed just $6.49 each in the U.S. or $6.74 each in Canada. That is a savings of at least 16% off the cover price. It's quite a bargain! Shipping and handling is just 50¢ per book in the U.S. and $1.25 per book in Canada.* I understand that accepting the 2 free books and gift places me under no obligation to buy anything. I can always return a shipment and cancel at any time by calling the number below. The free books and gift are mine to keep no matter what I decide.

Choose one:
☐ **Love Inspired Larger-Print**
(122/322 BPA GRPA)

☐ **Love Inspired Suspense Larger-Print**
(107/307 BPA GRPA)

☐ **Or Try Both!**
(122/322 & 107/307 BPA GRRP)

Name (please print)

Address   Apt. #

City   State/Province   Zip/Postal Code

Email: Please check this box ☐ if you would like to receive newsletters and promotional emails from Harlequin Enterprises ULC and its affiliates. You can unsubscribe anytime.

Mail to the **Harlequin Reader Service:**
IN U.S.A.: P.O. Box 1341, Buffalo, NY 14240-8531
IN CANADA: P.O. Box 603, Fort Erie, Ontario L2A 5X3

Want to try 2 free books from another series? Call 1-800-873-8635 or visit www.ReaderService.com.

---

*Terms and prices subject to change without notice. Prices do not include sales taxes, which will be charged (if applicable) based on your state or country of residence. Canadian residents will be charged applicable taxes. Offer not valid in Quebec. This offer is limited to one order per household. Books received may not be as shown. Not valid for current subscribers to the Love Inspired or Love Inspired Suspense series. All orders subject to approval. Credit or debit balances in a customer's account(s) may be offset by any other outstanding balance owed by or to the customer. Please allow 4 to 6 weeks for delivery. Offer available while quantities last.

Your Privacy—Your information is being collected by Harlequin Enterprises ULC, operating as Harlequin Reader Service. For a complete summary of the information we collect, how we use this information and to whom it is disclosed, please visit our privacy notice located at corporate.harlequin.com/privacy-notice. From time to time we may also exchange your personal information with reputable third parties. If you wish to opt out of this sharing of your personal information, please visit readerservice.com/consumerchoice or call 1-800-873-8635. **Notice to California Residents**—Under California law, you have specific rights to control and access your data. For more information on these rights and how to exercise them, visit corporate.harlequin.com/california-privacy.

LIRLIS23